Ni Bóna
Na Coróin

A Collection of
American Short
Stories
2015

Edited by
Diana Kathryn
Plopa

Grey Wolfe Publishing, LLC
PO Box 1088
Birmingham, Michigan 48009
www.GreyWolfePublishing.com

© 2015 Grey Wolfe Publishing, LLC
Published by Grey Wolfe Publishing, LLC
www.GreyWolfePublishing.com
All Rights Reserved

ISBN: 978-1628280852
Library of Congress Control Number: 2015942653

Ni Bona Na Coroin

A Collection of American Short Stories

2015

Edited by Diana Kathryn Plopa

The Grey Wolfe Publishing motto is *"Ni Bóna Na Coróin", which means "Neither Crown Nor Collar"*; and it symbolizes our commitment to the writers who come to us. We treat writers as equals, neither ruling over them, nor being subservient to them, as they fulfil their publishing dreams. We also believe that this sentiment embodies the True American Spirit. We are a people who place emphasis on our commonalities rather than our differences, and we work together as equals to solve problems, entertain, and research new avenues of discovery.

To celebrate this spirit of equality that we all share, Grey Wolfe Publishing hosted an American Short Story Competition. A portion of the proceeds from the sale of this book go to support the work of *The Intrepid Fallen Heroes Fund*, which serves United States Military personnel wounded or injured in service to our nation, and their families.

Ni Bóna Na Coróin.

Acknowledgements

The production of this book could not be accomplished without the expertise, literary passion and dedication of our amazing Pack. Each is a writer as well as a company team member; and each lends their unique perspective to serve both the company and our authors with integrity and creativity. We are grateful for their daily contributions to the growth of the Pack.

Editor's Note

This book is the result of a juried writing contest. All entries published within are presented exactly as they were submitted, without editorial changes.

Contents

The Confession
Christopher Chagnon

A rowdy western wind tried to tear the screen door from Floyd Meadow's hand when he let the bobcat in his house. No chance of that. He was still much too strong to let the wind have its way with the door. The bobcat had been holing up with Floyd for near on a month in his cabin at the end of Loomis Road. The bobcat's personality fit Floyd's like a marriage made in the wilderness; cantankerous, bold, mean but graceful, and they could piss wherever they wished. Yes, Floyd, and the bobcat were a lot alike. That's why they lived together on the dead-end road where he rarely had visitors; not because of the bobcat, Floyd didn't like visitors.

The force of the wind changed and pushed the screen door closed. He didn't fight the wind this time. Floyd remained peering through the plexiglass window watching the snow fill Father Arnie Stuben's footprints, and obscure the windshield of the priest's Chrysler van. His breath fogged the window during the seconds he studied the van, and his front yard swamp filling with snow. When the fog became impenetrable to his vision, he dragged a finger through the fog, and made a circled symbol, "Peace."

Father Stuben sat frozen to a high-backed cat-clawed chair. At his feet stood the bobcat. The bobcat had taken to Stuben's cassock covered legs like it was catnip, rubbing, arching its back, repeating his motions in a figure eight.

The priest sat motionless while the bobcat claimed him.

"Floyd?" Stuben let out a meek but desperate plea.

"Just let him do his thing, he'll quit sooner or later, once he figures he's got you marked enough," Floyd said, departing from the entry door to the one room cabin. "Just don't make any sudden movements if he starts to hiss and snarl. Ya' know yer' in his chair?"

"Oh, I can move to another," Stuben said. The bobcat began to object with a hiss directed at the cassock-covered clergyman.

"Good idea, it took me a couple a fights with the damned thing before I figured out the chair was his."

Stuben leaned and rose, and searched the room for a suitable replacement. The bobcat took his place, and began purring contently.

"Sit by the stove," Floyd pointed to a cedar branch chair he had made that summer. Father Stuben followed his recommendation.

Floyd Meadow's one room cabin contained remnants of his past. Old photos of he and his Army buddies hung in dusty frames suspended unevenly on bent nails. The photos showed a different Floyd; a Floyd Meadow with broad shoulders, and thick arms, young, tight facial skin covering his distant stare; a youthful warrior's body. Unlike the photo on his current driver's license depicting an old Floyd. Old Floyd's skin sunk below his chin, a profound, protruding stomach searched past his waistband. His thick, black hair had departed years earlier, making his head as barren as the minute he was born. There was a photo of Floyd holding a M-60 machine gun on a blown-up Vietnam hilltop. An inscription was inked across the bottom, 'A Shau Valley-1968'. Another photo portrayed Floyd's face covered in white lather, and his hand dipping a shaving razor into a brown-water-filled helmet. He was smiling in that one. He had spent two tours in 'Nam. Couldn't get enough of it, until it dawned on him, "I want to see the world." So he enlisted in the Navy, and set out to see it aboard the *USS Oriskany*. Further along the dingy wall were photos of him standing on a busy street in Cairo, Egypt; he was wearing a colorful turban, along with his evening whites. Bold. Brave. Drunk.

"May I?" the priest from St. Paul's parish, in Chandlerville asked. He left his chair to examine a cluster of souvenirs resting on a shelf below the photo display. He wanted to pick one up.

"Go ahead. Won't mean anything to you unless I tell you the story around it," Floyd said.

"What's the story on this one? Where did it come from?" Stuben asked, holding a rusted AK-47 bayonet.

"That one? It came from my shoulder after a dink shoved it in me. 1967, Quang Tri Provence."

Father Stuben held the blade closer to his eyes. No visible blood remained, but the time-embedded rust bore witness to its deadly use forty-seven years earlier. "What happened to the guy using it?"

"Huh," Meadow scoffed, and didn't provide an answer to the stupid question.

"Sorry, that was a dumb question," the priest cringed at his naiveté, and made the sign of the cross, but he continued with questions, "What happened after he stabbed you? I mean, other than the obvious?"

"I kept fightin'. The battle didn't stop after I got it. There were hundreds a' gooks ready to take his place, ready to finish us off. We kept fightin' because we had to." Floyd Meadow gave the priest an example, "Ever had the runs? The shits?"

Father Stuben jerked his head, "Well, yes, haven't we all? Why do you ask?"

"That's what it was like over there. Just when you think you're done, you got ta' go again. You got another wave comin' at ya', tearing yer' guts up. Then, when yer' tour is up, and you finally rotate, then you can wipe yer' ass. It's just that simple. I didn't get to wipe mine for two years. But then comes the shit sandwich."

Father Arnie Stuben returned the bayonet to the dust-traced silhouette where it had been laying for years, alongside Floyd's other war testaments. "Thank you for allowing me to come out here today, Floyd," Stuben said, returning to his chair. Before he sat he noticed two ruffed grouse lying in the porcelain sink. A loaded syringe was lying on the counter.

Floyd noticed him noticing, "The bobcat's a good hunter. He always brings back two of everything; one for him, and one for me."

"Amazing! The syringe? Diabetes?"

"Yes. I've had it for a number of years. I guess that's what can happen when you get drunk on every continent in the world. Thanks for reminding me." Floyd poked his finger, touched the trickle of blood on the tip of a monitor, and then emptied the syringe in his belly fat. "Your letter said you wanted to talk to me. What about, Father?" Floyd asked the priest.

Father Stuben hesitated by adjusting his clerical collar, and weaving his fingers together. He had been rehearsing what he would say to Floyd for decades. "You don't remember me, do you?"

Floyd studied the priest's humble, retreating, apologetic face, "No."

"June, 1969?"

"That's the month I returned home from 'Nam," Floyd recalled.

"I know. I was there. Royal Oak train station?"

"Yeah, Royal Oak, June 19, 1969, it wasn't pleasant, I remember. A horde of protesters met us when we walked out of the station. I was pelted with eggs, spit on, called a baby killer. I'll never forget it. That was my shit sandwich," Floyd continued, "I went to the nearest K-Mart and bought some civi's so I could get out of my uniform. I came back home, but I knew it was no place for me at that time. That's when I enlisted in the Navy."

"I was one of the protesters, Floyd." The priest reached inside his cassock, and produced the front page of a folded, frail newspaper. The masthead read, THE ROYAL OAK TRIBUNE. It was dated June 20, 1969. There was Floyd, egg embryo dripping from his Army uniform, his left arm raised in an attempt to shield his face from the next throw.

Floyd focused on the image. "Rotten eggs." He studied the front-page photo more closely. A slightly out of focus young man, holding an egg in his cocked arm, was jeering hatefully in the background. It was Arnie Stuben.

"Yes, that's me," the withering priest confessed. "I was a Political Science student at the University of Michigan, and had joined the SDS, Students for a Democratic Society. I thought I was doing the right thing back then. But when my younger brother, Rick, was killed in Vietnam later that year, my outlook on the war changed. I learned a young girl, who had concealed a grenade in her clothes, killed him. She pulled the pin while my brother was passing out Hershey Bars to other children. Rick and his Company were giving humanitarian relief to a village that had been hit hard by the Cong."

"I saw it happen all over the country, Father. Gook women and children could be as deadly as any man. Women, especially."

The bobcat began to stir on his perch, as though the conversation was boring him. He leaped to the floor and waited by the door. Floyd let him out where the snow was building into pillows on leafless tree branches. "He wants to hunt again. That's the amazing thing about a wild animal. They have no remorse when they kill. It's their nature. I believe it's man's nature, too, given the right circumstances."

"What do you mean, Floyd?"

"When I went in the Army, I was just a kid living in northern Michigan. I never wanted to kill anyone. But, I was trained to kill. When I got over there, and got into my first firefight, it all came into place. Like I was given a missing ingredient I didn't possess, a gear that was put into my motor to make me do what they wanted me to do, all of us. When yer' buried in a fox hole, and tracers are zinging over your head, and your buddy next to you gets it in the face and buys the farm, and you just had a beer with him the night before, and he showed you a photo of his sweetheart, and he's crying for his momma to save him, and now he's going back home to her in a box. That's when the gear takes hold. You want revenge, and it doesn't matter who they are. You just eliminate them the best way you can. Mamason, papason, babyson, they were all the enemy."

The priest listened, and understood. He wondered if his brother, Rick, would feel the same, were he still alive. "I never knew it was that bad, until Rick was killed. I had a long talk with his military escort. He was in Rick's Company, and there when it happened. We talked all night. That's when I decided I wanted to go into the priesthood." Father Stuben re-weaved his hands in front of his elbowed knees, "The Lord works mysteriously, Floyd. When I became the priest at St. Paul's, and found out you were living here, I knew it was all God's plan. I had to find you. I am here to make my confession, and ask your forgiveness." The priest bent to his knees, and began to weep.

Floyd Meadow stood beside the tormented Father Stuben. He placed a comforting hand on the priest's shoulder, "I have to show you something." Floyd walked to the shelf that held his history. He removed a small metal canister that had remained sealed since the day he left Vietnam. Floyd opened the container, and removed what was inside. It was his dog tags from Vietnam. But threaded on the chain hung something else; a brown, leathery piece of flesh, an ear he had severed from a Viet Cong enemy. "Just as you have kept the newspaper, I have kept this. I have been waiting for the right time to make absolution, Father." Floyd walked to the wood stove, opened the door and tossed his dog tags onto the burning coals. "The ear belonged to a young boy I killed." He returned to the priest, went to his knees, and begged, "Father, forgive me, for I have sinned. It has been a lifetime since my last confession."

The priest and the old soldier wept and prayed. Each forgave the other.

There came a summons at the cabin door, it was the bobcat. Floyd wiped his tears, rose stiffly from his knees, and let the bobcat in. The bobcat was carrying two rabbits in its jaws. One was an adult snowshoe rabbit; the other was a young baby rabbit. Once again, the wild animal provided for he and Floyd.

The bobcat never asked for forgiveness, it was his nature to kill.

Walk The Steel
Dennis Klotz

Across the East River, on the Brooklyn side, Kwite and his brothers looked across to Manhattan. The city scintillated in the hot night, a big glowing metropolis, murmurous with the humming of a new and alien modernity. Kwite had never seen anything like it before. It felt strange and foreign. He had come with his brothers, Danyen and Atonwa, down from their Mohawk home in Akwesasne, near the St. Lawrence River, to be part of a rivet gang on the new buildings that were going up in Manhattan, the ones they called skyscrapers.

It was his first night in New York, and they would start early the next morning, heading across the Brooklyn Bridge into Manhattan where the steel and the work would await them. Danyen and Atonwa could barely contain their restlessness and they chatted excitedly amongst themselves late into the night. But Kwite could not sleep. It was not due to Danyen and Atonwa's talking, but rather a sharp sense of unease that Kwite felt within himself. He tossed and turned in his bunk and tried to think of their last night at Akwesasne.

Danyen and Atonwa had asked their father to tell them stories about his time working on the Victoria Bridge over the St. Lawrence River. The Mohawks were promised work since the bridge ran through their reservation, and they soon began climbing it after their shifts ended. He and the other boys would challenge each other to go higher, in order to prove their courage and their manhood. It was the lure of danger and death that excited him, as well as a deep pride and a restlessness he felt in pursuing the climb. He was fearless, poised, graceful and statuesque as he walked the narrow beams, high above the churning river as the other men watched in awe, holding their breath, bracing themselves for a fall which never came. Amazed at his deftness and his seeming fearlessness, he was trained as a riveter along with other the Mohawks who showed similar skill and bravery in high places. Danyen and Atonwa loved hearing these stories, and they couldn't wait to go to New York City to help build these giant steel buildings and prove their courage. They would leave the following day for the city to join their uncle on a new building that was under way in Manhattan. Danyed and Atonwa were very eager to see the city, after hearing stories about it from their uncle. He spoke of the people, the vastness, and the magnificence of it. It was one of the largest cities in the world, he said. And he said it was growing; outwards and upwards. The upwards part fascinated Atonwa and Danyen, and they couldn't wait to see these buildings that grew to the sky. Mostly, they were excited to work with their uncle and carry on the tradition their father had started, that of displaying great courage and agility, of building things one could take pride in, that of walking the steel. Danyen and Atonwa talked with their father as the night wore on, but Kwite had been silent for most of the night. He didn't share their lively energy, but his silence carried more weight than he hoped to let on.

When Kwite was just a boy he had been climbing a tall elm with Danyen. Kwite had climbed ahead, and when he called back to Danyen, there was no answer. Kwite looked down, and saw he was higher up than he realized. He looked out and saw Danyen scampering back through the forest. Kwite called again, his voice higher in a panic, but Danyen did not hear him. The earth looked so far below him, and Kwite, in his trepidation, felt a sharp lightness in all his limbs before the world went dark. Kwite awoke at the foot of the great elm, sore from the fall, and plunged his fingers into the soft earth, glad to be down from the tree, and to have solid ground underfoot.

Kwite never spoke of that time in the tree to anyone, but every time his father spoke of his feats during the construction of the Victoria Bridge and later, on the Soo Bridge over the St. Mary's

Ni Bona Na Coroin

River, he thought again of the tree and of his fear.

Now, as Kwite lay alongside his brothers in the lodging house in Brooklyn, he was nervous about what the next day would bring. He closed his eyes and prayed for strength and courage. Kwite fell asleep thinking about the tree.

The morning sun washed over Manhattan and the city was already bustling with the sounds of trolleys, of paper boys selling The Herald, The Times, Harper's Weekly, and Collier's. As they walked through the lower east side, they heard many languages being spoken at once, and it seemed as if the whole city was speaking in tongues, above the cacophony of the urban jangle. Already women were out with their parasols, shopping, passing by messenger boys and horse drawn carriages, passing merchants selling cured meats and wares of all kinds. The city rumbled and hummed, and as they neared the construction site, the rumble grew louder.

The three of them stood looking skyward at the half completed building in front of them. It was taller and more impressive than they had imagined. Kwite felt the fear already. Three hours later they were working alongside their uncle, on the fifty sixth floor, Atonwa tossing the rivets to Kwite who hammered them into place. Each minute seemed like an eternity for Kwite who was trying not to look down or up or around, just focusing on securing the rivets into their place.

At mid-day, when they changed positions, Kwite knew he had to cross the gap to where Atonwa was. He looked down at the narrow beam of steal before him and felt his hands grow moist and his heart beating faster as he placed one foot in front of the other. Kwite felt the first twinge of fright, a cold column of terror running through him. The beam jutted out over the city, over the streets where people walked below like ants, utterly oblivious to the pounding of steel, the screwing of rivets, the tap dance of balance which meant life or death, that took place nearly sixty stories above their heads, high enough where the drones of hammers and rivets became just another noise in the endless hum of the future city muscling its way into Manhattan.

Kwite felt the lightness in his limbs again and he knew he was half way across when he felt the rush of wind against his skin, and heard Atwone yelling, but he couldn't make out the words. He saw his foot slip, and the steel beam coming closer to his face. He had no time to react, and his arms and hands clutched instinctively to the beam. His face was close to the beam and his shaking hands, and Kwite did not look up when he felt the hand tugging at him, only heard the screaming and then saw Atwone's scared face passing by him as he fell to the street below.

Kwite's fear was gone now, replaced by a sharp pain in his heart, an ominous emptiness and a cold, numbing shock. He walked the rest of the way in a trance, into Danyen's arms who grabbed him firmly. He could not make out what Danyen or his uncle were screaming. He didn't want to hear.

He and Danyen left the next day to take Atwone's body back to Akwesasne for burial. Danyen would not talk to Kwite, and Kwite knew that it was his fear that was to blame for Atwone. Danyen knew it too.

After Atwone was put back to the earth, and after Danyen had gone to sleep, Kwite stayed awake with his father in the long house.

"You were afraid my son," his father said.

"Yes father, I was afraid," said Kwite. "I'm to blame for what happened to Atwone. He was the one trying to save me. It happened so quickly," he said between tears.

"I am sorry father. I never want to lessen our name, where we come from, who we are. But I'm not like you. You know that. I'm scared father. So scared every day. That city..." he said looking towards the creek. "When will it ever end? Day and night they build it higher. I never get a rest from the noise. It's not like how it was for grandfather, or our ancestors. Every night I dream of a peaceful forest, one without cities, one before they came."

His father looked at him a long while and did not speak, just let the fire crackle and the haunting hooting of a loon ring out in the night.

"My father built canoes. He hunted those woods where the bridge now is and brought fur to the traders so our people could grow strong. So they could survive. He dreamed of those woods too, the ones his forefathers knew." He looked at the dying fire, it's glow diminishing, the wood logs turning gray and ashen. " But we don't get to go back, Kwite. We only get to go as far as we can, for our sons and our son's sons."

"But when does it stop?"

"It won't.," he said, looking east towards New York. "They'll never stop." he said shaking his head. "It will never stop." He took his stick and stoked the fire more, the last few embers popping and dying out. "But we are a part of it now. We'll endure."

Kwite and his father stared at the fire not speaking, listening to the night, the forest whispering with wildlife and wonder.

Kwite did not go back to the city that summer, and he stayed at Akwesasne thinking of Atwone, and thinking of the great elm, and dreaming. Kwite longed for a time before the Dutch, before the French and the Jesuits, a time before this new bold nation that was growing bigger and bigger every day. He longed for the quietness of the forest. He longed for wampum belts and drums, and song flutes at sunset, when the night meant a sleeping world and not one that roars continuously with teeming urban life. Kwite longed for the calm still waters, the elms and the pines, dugout canoes and good fishing in the streams.

His father saw this longing, and talked again with him by the fire.

"Do you remember what we used to call you as a boy?"

"Akweks," Kwite said.

"Yes, Akweks," his father said. "Eagle. Do you remember the myth that was your favorite as a boy? The one about the boy who turned into an eagle?"

"Yes," Kwite said. "The one of He Who Walks A Different Path. He became an Eagle, a symbol of Truth and Freedom for all those who see it."

"Yes, Kwite," said his father. "But eagles are not afraid. You cannot have Freedom if you are afraid and you cannot know truth. You must endure, like the boy did. You must conquer your fear."

Kwite thought about what his father said and prayed very deeply for four days, before deciding to return to work with Danyen and his uncle in the city.

When he arrived, they were working on another building, this one bigger than the one he first worked on. As he climbed up, he felt the lightness in his limbs again. He thought of the tree and of Atwone. Kwite's heart began to race again, but he thought of what his father told him and he climbed up, higher and higher to where Danyen and his uncle were. He stared down at the beam again, narrow and dizzying sevety five stories above the street. He walked out, one foot in front of the other, the blood rushing from his face, his nerves like hot bolts. Kwite caught his breath, held it, and breathed out again. He looked back and realized he had walked the steel the full length. Danyen gave a smug nod of approval before tossing him a rivet.

Three months later, Kwite walked out on the beam, the skyscraper nearly complete and looked out over Manhattan towards the East River and to Brooklyn and Queens beyond. The air seemed different up there, the whole city seemed different. He thought of the myths his father told him as a child, of the boy and the eagle.

Kwite stood, proud on the smooth steel, the girder light under his feet, his fears vanquished. He looked out over the city. He had never looked at it before. It looked beautiful and vibrant in the afternoon sun. It looked the way an eagle would view it. Kwite knew then that his father was right. His people, his traditions, this great steel giant he helped erect, and the people down below who lived in its shadow; all of it would endure. He would make sure of it.

Real Time
Shannon Waite

Well, first things first. Let me tell you one way that the American Dream is never shown: in the snow.

My Levi's low on my waist, I laid on the dock, offering myself to the American sun that was glazing my already tanned skin. It was a hotter than hot Michigan July day, and I felt mildly bold next to the water that was covered in those brilliant reflections that always seem to get caught on top.

The daylight engulfed me and I didn't fight it.

To be honest, I didn't fight much of anything anymore. The world was so busy pushing me around all of the time. I found myself just giving in to it all, which was new to me because I had always been a fighter, but I couldn't do it anymore. It was easier to give in.

"Brandon!" I squealed as you picked me up, arms tight around my waist, begging to throw me into the lake. I kicked my legs, trying to control your balance, but you were so much stronger than me and nothing I did was going to stop you.

"Please don't throw me in!"

You laughed at me, just like the rest of our friends who were standing there and watching us were laughing at me, and with one great force you pushed me away from you.

My breath escaped quickly as I felt my feet hit the water first; an explosion beneath my body welcomed me as my weight sunk me lower and lower while I scrambled to pull myself up. After what felt like forever and wet hair, I emerged with a gasp and a group of six was still watching me and laughing.

I saw an arm stretch out to me. You leaned down with your hand. I accepted it and climbed back up.

It was easier to give in than it was to fight it, remember?

The summer afternoon of popsicles, hula hoops, and tire swings transitioned into evening where everything calmed down as my hair dried out and the sun kissed the sky goodnight. Surrounding me was the stale kind of air; the kind of air that holds no temperature at all and just lets you be. It did hold fireflies though, and those flickered in and out of realization as the seven of us sat around the campfire.

Silently, I delved through thoughts. Thoughts of this group of friends when we first met in seventh grade; thoughts of summer trips up to this cottage together; thoughts of how foreign owning a cottage was to me, because even though you were always inviting us up here, this was something my family never had.

"So, Lindsey," Michelle said to me from across the fire as the shadows and orange glow highlighted her face.

Pulled from my thoughts, I nodded my head in response.

"Where have you decided to go to school in the fall?"

Oh. I sat still. Huddled up, knees to my chest, concealed in the overly large foldable camping chair. I evaded the question for a moment.

"Uh," I mumbled, thinking of how to respond. Was it bad that I hadn't planned that far yet?

"Come on, Girl! Where have you been? " She mocked me. As much as it hurt, she was right. School started in less than two months and I had not yet been accepted anywhere. Although I considered the possibility, I denied to myself that I wouldn't be going to any college, but I think that the reality of the situation was beginning to set in; I wasn't going.

Just like yours, Michelle's family had also been well off. I can't say that she understood where my family came from, so of course to her it seemed unfortunate that I wasn't already enrolled in a college. That was just expected in her family.

"It'll happen soon," I shrugged.

Flash forward to three AM: it's after all of the midnight hikes, and jumps in the lake, and burnt out fires; the rest of the troop was letting the late nights of the week catch up to them, but I was still wide awake and inflamed with every impossibility that I was facing.

"What's going on, Lindsey?"

The rest of the group laid halfway-mostly-on-top of each other, scattered across the spaces available in the cottage living room. That's where we usually crashed when we came up here. It was fun as a kid, but this hapless sleepover system was really kind of uncomfortable now. No more than twenty feet away from them, on the front porch, you and I sat underneath the rainstorm of stars set above us.

"What d'you mean?"

"You!" you spurted. "Something's up with you and it ain't cool."

I nervously sucked on my lip. "I don't know what you're talking about."

I felt mosquitoes collecting at the base of my ankle. I swatted at them. I purposely let myself get caught in the distraction.

"Damnit, Lindsey, stop it. I want you to pay attention."

Drizzled galaxies; singing crickets; dusty bare feet.

I looked up from the ground. You never talked to me like that—not usually, anyways. I stopped. The bugs weren't my biggest concern anymore.

"What is it, Brandon?" Exasperated.

You sat on my left and, putting your right elbow on your knee, you leaned closer in to me.

"I just want to know what's going on."

Crickets filled the awkward spaces now—kind of like punctuation does in a sentence. You stopped shifting your weight forward and waited for my response. I wasn't giving one. The porch light reflected against your eyes. Your hair was getting kind of scraggly now, like the surfer style, except being in Michigan you didn't surf. It was hanging in your face the way that lake-wet hair dries kind of stringy-like. You weren't wearing a shirt because it was still warm outside, even after dark, and that tan that you gathered during the day lay on your skin so well.

"I don't know what you're talking about," I replied. I wasn't going to fight it much longer.

With split-second-quickness, you erupted, throwing your hands in the air and turning to kick the banister of the porch steps.

"I'm trying, Lindsey!" you yelled, "What else do you want me to do?"

Another knock against the banister, but this time from your fist.

Pressure; the pressure from an overwhelming force, moving forward, pushed against me. I imagine it's what it feels like when you're in a fire and that pressure is pushing against the windows that are about to shatter. This pressure wasn't from a normal fire though; this pressure was from some kind of internal flame.

Exhaling softly, my lifts parted as I faced you. I ran through my options. I ran through my list of lies.

A choice made, words said, "What are you doing in the fall, Brandon?"

"Going to CMU, but you know that—why the hell are you asking?"

I ignored your question.

"What am I doing in the fall, Brandon?"

Eyes narrowed, you suspiciously responded. "You're working on figuring out what school you want to go to."

Awkward pause.

You questioned me, "Right?"

"What happens if that doesn't happen? What happens if it doesn't work out? What happens if I haven't even been looking?"

What happens if other plans came up?

"You haven't been looking?"

Out of the three questions I verbally posed, you only responded to the last one. You lowered yourself back down to my level, once again sitting on the porch, and you rubbed your fist that was beginning to swell.

"Where could I even go?"

Your question was answered with another question and that was where the night came to a close.

As I rose with the sun that following morning, I found an interesting pattern of grids running along my arms.

I had ended up sleeping on the lawn.

"I love you, Linds. No matter what you choose to do," you whispered.

No matter what.

The night ended with a heavy sigh, a light kiss, and a weighty shadow that grew as you continued making your way towards the porch light.

Something about it all fused the need for an escape and the need to be alone together. The best thing I could come up with at that moment was sleeping in a space that was free from you and everyone else; a space where there were no restrictions; a space that was organic. The best space available was, ultimately, the lawn and as a result the thing that I learned that night was that grass leaves lines.

One step, two step, three step; I reached up to carefully climb the ladder hanging from the oak tree at the front of the forest. This area had very few of these trees, but this one lay rooted in the soil behind the cabin. It was so big that I couldn't even look up at it without craning my head all the way back to get the highest branch in my line of vision.

Close to five years ago we decided that this would be the perfect tree for a tree house. After much persuading, persuading meaning begging and pleading, your parents gave in and built us our own tree house—but of course they did. Man, this thing was brilliant.

We spent so many nights curled up in the corners of it under blankets, and making up stupid stories and even dumber jokes. We were kids then though; now, we were high school graduates. Some of us, you, for example, were going to be starting college soon. Back then was different.

In that moment however, I didn't feel too different anymore which is why I was climbing the tree. This time it would be alone though, which I don't think I had ever done before.

For two hours I sat on what felt like the horizon of my life, gazing at the Earth's horizon below me: unmanageable forestry, wild grassland, cluttered trees, and mildly calm waves.

I sat there, thinking about how you, and Michelle, and most of everyone else there that week, grew up in lifestyles vastly different from mine. Even though we could all play together, sit around a campfire together, and pack into a cottage living room to sleep together, we were not anything like each other.

I had a mother, a father, and a younger sister, so, a family I guess you could call it, but my family had almost no money. Especially no money like you guys. Dad was a gambling addict and Mom couldn't find work. As I was growing up, I was lucky we stayed in the same apartment sometimes.

I guess this was a story I had never told you. It didn't have a happy ending and no one wants to hear those kinds of stories.

My family and I lived in the same house as my grandmother and, as far as you were concerned, Grandma lived with us. That wasn't quite the situation though; really, we lived with Grandma. After Dad lost the rest of our savings one night at the tables, we had nowhere else to go once we lost our house too. We didn't lose the house though, really. I knew exactly where it was, we just no longer owned it. We couldn't live in it.

You never knew this life. Michelle never knew this life. None of you guys did. Not as far as I knew, anyways. I tried too hard to hide it.

One step, two step, three step. I heard the suggestions of your arrival.

"Lindsey?"

My feet had been hanging from the opening but I pulled them in and scooted to the right so that you had space to join me.

"What're you doin' up here?" With one last push you clambered inside, regained your composure, and pulled yourself into the gap next to me.

"What am I ever doing up here?"

Another question answered with a question.

"Escaping," you replied thoughtfully.

We sat in silence for a moment, both facing the same horizon, although I'm not sure that we saw the same thing.

"So... no matter what?" My voice was quiet and even. It needed to be, in this kind of instance. This time wasn't like the times when we were kids and laughing and joking and telling stories up in the tree house. This time, we were actually making a story, which was much more than simply telling one.

"What'd you mean?"

I turned from the horizon ahead of me in order to face you on the left of me. You already forgot.

"...You said that you'd love me—no matter what I chose to do."

"Oh, yeah—of course." Your voice matched mine; it too was quiet and even.

I gave you a half-hearted smile. The other half of it was guts.

My emotions felt scrambled, like I was fingering the pages of a picture-flip book; each page a slightly adjusted image, letting me observe a small animation of something like a bike cycling, a bunny hopping, or a heart breaking.

Words. I collected the words dwelling inside of me and began to piece them together when we both started speaking at the same time.

After stopping midsentence, you said "Lindsey—just go."

Breaths inhaled deeply began to make me feel dizzy. I considered what I was about to say.

"Okay," I began, "can I tell you something?"

You were frustrated. You nodded your head.

I pushed through walls of everything I wanted to escape; I didn't need to sleep on the lawn to feel free. I realized that I could have done that anywhere, even in the cottage living room. What I needed was to break the barrier I was barricading myself with. I needed to take the stance of a fighter again, like old times, because while giving in was easy, it also felt hard as hell.

"I'm terrified" I stated.

With no response from you I paused. You remained quiet. Birds in the trees around us filled the silence as I felt my words tripping me up.

"About what?" you said when I didn't get myself uncaught from the web of panic that I was in.

I didn't know how to say it. I repeated myself. "I'm terrified."

Thwap, flick, flutter. You blinked at me. You blinked at me a few times in a row and your right eyebrow started to rise.

I gathered the bits and pieces and parts of the sentence I was about to tell you, sat up uncomfortably straight, and felt the words tumble from my mouth.

One more time, "I'm terrified..." You can do it, just finish the damn sentence - "and I'm pregnant."

The eyebrow dropped. Your eyes narrowed. Deep breath.

Pound, pound, pound. Thud, thud, thud. I felt like I was going to implode.

"I'm sorry," I whispered quietly; so quiet that it rested under my breath and I wasn't even sure you had heard it. My eyes had already fallen but now my head followed. My heart was coming next.

Deep breath.

As I began to inhale, I felt your arms loop around me and pull me in like a tornado. Typically, tornados only last for a few minutes.

In the eye of the storm, I buried my face in your still-shirtless-shoulder.

The sweet summer air was growing warmer; our sticky bodies made it worse. Then, after what seemed like less than a minute of our bodies touching, as quickly as the tornado came, it vanished too.

Your body straightened up and your shoulders evened out. I knew what you were about to ask and I didn't want to hear it.

"So," you started, "what's the plan then?"

I half-way scoffed. Screw you. I didn't have a plan; I didn't have an answer; as of right now, I had almost nothing other than my life, this infant's life, and the remnants of what I once knew as your life before all of these changes.

I don't know directions, but I knew that this conversation was not going in one that I wanted. In response, I changed the subject. Yes, I knew that this wasn't going to go away, but I also knew that it wasn't a question and it therefore didn't need to be answered. Not right then. I also knew that you'd follow my lead and drop the subject.

In response to you I shrugged.

"What were you going to say before this? When we started at the same time?" I fumbled. Avoidance.

"Oh..." You paused before finishing. "I was going to ask when you were going to leave the tree house..."

Later that night I sat by myself in the grass again. The way my head spun made it feel like the world was out of control. I knew that it wasn't what was out of control, but feeling that way took a little of the pressure off of me.

A firefly fluttered past me and I watched as its glow dimmed then disappeared. Fireflies use light to communicate, you know. Also, some fireflies eat other fireflies. They're cannibals. It was no longer shining so I lost site of the bug.

Sitting alone, I faced no fear as I hopelessly reached for

time.

I clung to anticipation.

I held onto everything that others might mock me for as I rested uncertainly between the depths of that summer. In that moment, I had no idea what was in store for me, that was sure.

One thing I did know though, it's never shown in snow, but it was in that kind of place where the American Dream is shown.

And under the eternal summer sun, I let the world touch me. That would be the last time though because now, I was going to start fighting back once more. My skin was thick, and I was not going to let myself find grass lines on it ever again.

Actually, Minnesota Has Three Nicknames
Melissa Grunow

Ray knew she was nervous. He glanced at her while she stared out the car window, her forehead pressed against the slightly fogged glass. He could hear her breathing; her lips grazed the window. Even when he was concentrating on the thick Minneapolis traffic, he couldn't ignore the way she wrapped a section of her long, dark hair around her index finger, tugging it hard enough to pull her skin away from the glass, her head bobbing, then falling silently back against the window.

"The roads are strange here," Marla said without turning her head. "All the signs are different colors, and the exits are really confusing. And over there," she pressed her fingertip to the window, "those houses look like they fell out of the sky, like some kid just dropped them there. It would be hard trying to get used to a place like this, don't you think?" She crossed her legs, pressing her toe into the dashboard and scratched the back of her calve through her jeans.

He looked at her and smiled. He knew she wasn't trying to be critical, so he had stopped assuming how she felt and just let her talk. "At least you don't have to drive," he said. "This is the worst time of the day." He placed his hand on her knee and squeezed it.

She pulled away without looking at him. "Don't do that. Don't tickle."

"Sorry." Ray unfolded the piece of paper lying on his knee, and squinted at the handwritten directions, second-guessing his memory. He had been through this city before, about every six months or so, but everything was always changing. The buildings always seemed taller and closer together, the exits marked differently. On any other trip, he would rely on Marla to direct him. She liked to plan ahead, to feel in control, and he liked to watch her work—her reading glasses slipping down on her nose, a road atlas open across her lap. She loved to read maps, but hated to drive in unfamiliar places. He trusted her instinct with directions, especially because it took the pressure off of him. And she always apologized if she advised an incorrect turn, which was rare, and she could formulate a backup plan quickly enough so they would never lose too much time. After all, Marla refused to arrive anywhere late.

On the plane they had traveled in virtual silence with their knees resting comfortably against each other. Ray's ears were covered with headphones as he flipped through an old issue of Men's Health, while Marla's glasses reflected light onto the pages of a Grisham novel. She loved popular novels for their predictable plots and unified endings. The ones she really liked—where the heroine reunites with her estranged mother or the teenager gives up drugs to pursue a college education—she stacked in the back of her closet, their spine against the wall, next to a pile of cookbooks filled with recipes for dishes from around the world. Her mother had bought one for her for Christmas every year since Marla was sixteen, hoping she would be overtaken by the urge to cook. Yet, Marla still preferred a salad or vegetable soup and oyster crackers to sizzling fajitas or sashimi and rice, her simplistic approach to everything mimicked by her eating habits.

Marla pulled her head away from the glass and turned her body so she couldn't help to face Ray. "No, I'm sorry. I don't mean to be jumpy." She traced the stitching in the seat with her fingers, picking at the cigarette burns with her jagged, unkempt nails. Ray knew Marla didn't even own nail polish. She didn't like how it smelled.

"You all right?" He wanted to watch her reaction, but didn't want to miss the exit. He caught her nodding in his peripheral vision. Ray wanted her to say something, anything. He was even grateful for her comments about the misplaced houses and the strange highway.

"I think so." She tilted her head backward, looked at him, and smiled.

Marla's personality was direct and intense, and she had the ability to intimidate and fascinate at the same time. People feared her and admired her, questioned her and became enthralled with her. When Ray and Marla had first met, before she even spoke, Ray was drawn to her seriousness, and how everything she did, every word she spoke, felt real and natural, until it seemed she had always been there in one form or another.

Ray grinned back and winked. "You nervous?" His tone was quiet and serious, and he held his breath as he watched Marla shift her weight. She started to pull on her hair again. "Because it's okay, you know. I would be, too."

She sucked the thick, heavy air of the rental car through her teeth, and exhaled with a nonchalant, "Maybe a little."

"It's going to be fine." Ray wrapped his hand around her knee and gave it a light squeeze. "He'll love you, I swear. He's just that kind of kid."

She nodded as she put her head back against the window to watch the skyline shift, the hotels duck out of sight behind department stores and corporate offices.

"Where are we meeting them again?" She was staring out the window, talking just to make noise. She did that sometimes, like she was avoiding silence.

He glanced at the directions again. Like the gaining familiarity of the streets, Stephanie's handwriting curved along the notebook paper in front of him. "Stuart Anderson's. It's just a few miles from their house. Apparently, it's famous for its baked potato soup." Ray tried to manipulate his voice so his memory of the restaurant wasn't questioned. He didn't want to tell Marla the last time he had been there, the first time, was when he had followed Stephanie to Minnesota, begged her to try again, to give the relationship, and Ray, another chance. He didn't want Marla to know or to picture him begging another woman to stay in his life, especially when that other woman was someone he rarely thought about now.

Marla looked over at the directions and scowled. She had been left out of the planning. From the kitchen of their small apartment, Marla had listened to the strengthening and softening of Ray's voice on the telephone in their bedroom. Together, Ray and Stephanie decided to meet at a restaurant so Marla could meet both James and his mom. And together, Ray and Stephanie had decided it would be fun for James to stay at the hotel with Marla and Ray. Marla had never been consulted, never been asked, and Ray knew not talking to her was a mistake, but he wasn't accustomed to making those kinds of decisions with anyone.

He had never brought any of his past girlfriends on this trip before, but Marla was different; Marla was worth it. When the two of them were alone together, out to dinner or reclining on their couch and watching '80s Brat Pack movies, they made sense. When they were together, alone, they were strong, and her face never lied to him, never gave false impressions. He wanted her to be ready for this part of him, but he didn't know for sure if she was.

Marla's forehead relaxed and her face grew softer, longer. "I feel like I should hate her, and I don't even know her." She squished her face against the glass, and brought her knees into the door, so when Ray looked at her, all he could see was the sharp curve of her back, bending itself into her legs.

Ray tightened his fists around the steering wheel and sighed quietly, just loud enough for him to feel the frustration expel from his nostrils, but too quiet to get Marla's attention. He almost hated her when she acted like this, as if she were shutting him down, not allowing him to defend himself and without willingness to forgive.

"Marla." The radio was turned off, and the only sounds came from outside of the car, muffled by the closed windows and interrupted by Ray's voice. "Marla, look at me. Please."

She turned her head slightly, and when her eyes met Ray's profile, he felt them relax slightly. Her body eased, and her knees fell away from the door.

"There's no hate here. There's nothing. Just James." Ray felt tired, drained of explanation, drained of answers that weren't good enough.

She narrowed her eyes at him. Ray knew she wanted to dispute his assumption, but she didn't want to fight. He watched the suspicion slip down her face until her cheeks relaxed and her jaw unclenched itself. He knew she was trying to imagine the day Stephanie announced she was moving out and taking James with her. Ray knew Marla assumed he hadn't tried to stop her, which was only partly true. They had been living together, but Stephanie had been gone for months. Some nights she would go out, leave Ray with James and not return until Ray had to leave for work the next day. He couldn't stop Stephanie from leaving any more than he could stop Marla from preparing herself for looking his past in the eyes, possibly even shaking its hand. Marla always was thinking, always anticipating, always worrying and wondering about what may come next.

Ray looked across the car seat at the woman sitting with a strong, confident posture, staring straight ahead. At least she wasn't looking away from him, though she still wasn't looking directly at him, either.

"Are you hungry?" he asked her as he examined the directions again.

"I could eat." She wrapped the end of her hair around her finger and started tugging again. She typically didn't like to eat in front of people she didn't know, and Ray was a little surprised, and a little grateful, for her effort. She thought eating was something intimate, and she only did it around people she trusted.

"This state is called the Land of 10,000 Lakes," Marla said aloud, as though she were speaking only to herself.

"Is that right?" Ray felt hopeful she was starting to relax, to notice things that didn't merit criticism, only innocent observation.

"That's what all the license plates say. Look," she pointed to the pickup truck in front of them, "across the bottom. Land of 10,000 Lakes. I haven't really seen any lakes, though. Only buildings and strange roads." Her tone was serious, and it made him want to smile at her. Her inquisitiveness was cute, almost childlike, and it was when brief moments of her innocence like this overcame her outward strength that he felt like he was the only person in the world who mattered, like her observation was a sacred code, a form of confidence only between them; the rest of the world oblivious. This was how he had imagined this trip, this was how he had imagined they would connect, would have to connect, his only opportunity to prove to himself that she mattered to him, too.

"No, I can't imagine you would be able to see any lakes from the highway. Not with all the development here," Ray waved his hand, indicating both sides of the street. "Maybe more up north, in the suburbs. And we're not too far from Wisconsin, so there's a lot to Minnesota that you haven't seen."

"Do you know how much longer?" She rolled her shoulders back, and cracked her neck.

"Maybe twenty minutes," Ray told her. "It's hard to say."

"You said you've been here before." She didn't turn to look at him, and Ray knew she was suddenly on the verge of picking a fight. Her moods could change like that sometimes—quick, small shifts, and the results often were destructive, cutting. But Ray was unwilling to get burned this time, so he was careful to react.

"It was about a year ago. Cities change all the time, at least bigger cities like this one."

She sighed deeply. "Sounds hard to be so far away from a child for that long. He probably won't even look the same." She rested her head back against the window, closed her eyes, and stayed quiet. She was waiting for him to punch back, to throw his words like fists and let them give her a reason to defend herself. She wanted to make this his fault.

But Ray didn't respond, because part of him knew she was right, and part of him didn't want to argue with her just before they got to the restaurant. He, too, was starting to feel anxious, but he didn't tell Marla that, and he suspected she didn't care. He tried to ignore his disappointment that she had not once asked him what he was feeling. Seeing Stephanie made him remember all the anger she had caused him, all the hatred, all the disappointment. Ray would never admit it, but it was sometimes difficult for him to trust Marla, to wonder if she was really at work during the whole day, to wonder if he should go with her to the grocery store. He knew Marla didn't do the things Stephanie had, yet he couldn't get rid of his suspicions, and he could never tell her the truth about them. He was afraid she would blame him, and never be able to accept this part of his life.

"We're closer than I thought," Ray's voice finally broke the silence between them as he pointed to a sign. "The exit is in two miles."

"Do you know where to go from there?" Marla's shoulders were somewhat relaxed, her body shifted toward him.

"I have it written here." Ray held up the piece of paper with Stephanie's directions. "I kind of remember, but you know me. I'm better with landmarks than with reading street signs."

Marla reached for it. "Let me help you." She unfolded her hand, and placed her palm face up in the space between them. "It's getting dark. It might be hard to see, and we don't want to be late."

Fifteen minutes later, they pulled into a tiny parking lot, cracked and speckled with weeds and faded paint.

"You ready?" Ray cut the engine, the car wheezing itself to a rest after persistent stop-and-go driving.

He watched Marla open the door, and step out, her actions to be her only response. He walked around the trunk to her side of the car, and took her hand in his. He smiled at her, and watched her force a smiling nod back. "Are they here?" Marla asked, just as a young, wiry boy wearing Wranglers and a buttoned flannel shirt pushed through Stuart Anderson's heavy wooden door, followed by a thin, dark-haired woman. The boy started to run toward them but halted just before the walkway turned into asphalt. He looked down at his toes, then up, and knowing not to run through parking lots, started waving furiously. "Daddy!" The boy jumped up and down and squealed.

Ray quickened his pace, forgetting Marla was attached to him, and she fell a step behind, allowing herself to stumble and be dragged. Ray approached the sidewalk with his arms spread wide, and James jumped again as Ray scooped him up into a hug. For a single moment they were alone, reunited, missed time forgotten, only the future of one week together.

"Hi, Ray," the dark-haired woman said.

Ray looked at her and nodded, then looked around her shoulder for her husband. "Where's George?"

"George is bowling tonight, so it's just the four of us."

Ray turned behind him to face Marla who was silent, which made her look small, shriveled.

"You must be Marla." It was Stephanie who broke the trance, made Marla look up, stand up, and even smile.

Marla shook Stephanie's hand and turned to Ray as he set James back down on the sidewalk.

James looked at Marla, unblinking. "Are you my daddy's girl friend?"

"Let's go," Stephanie said. "Our table is ready."

Inside, the hostess lead them to a booth, and when Ray sat down, James scrambled up next to him, forcing Marla to sit with Stephanie. Ray tried to make eye contact with her to see if she was all right, but Marla hid behind her menu while James colored his paper placemat with red, blue, and green crayons.

"Watch, Dad, I can do this maze all by myself." James followed a path with his red crayon, drawing a circle around the star at the end. "See?"

"Very good." Ray put his arm around him and squeezed his shoulders. "Do you know what you want to eat?"

"How was your flight?" Stephanie's words seemed out of place and misdirected, as if she was talking to the booth as she dug through her purse.

Marla looked up at Ray who was reading the five-item children's menu. "It was fine. No lost luggage, no delays." Marla sipped from her water glass.

Stephanie nodded as she withdrew a crushed soft pack of Kools from her purse and flicked her lighter.

Ray noticed, and opened his mouth, but couldn't say anything. He looked at Marla. He knew it was coming. He knew she was waiting for something like this to happen.

"My mother died of emphysema. She got it from smoking." Marla said quietly, not looking at Stephanie. She studied the menu, pretending she was interested in the steaks or barbecue chicken dinners.

James looked up from his coloring, his gray eyes lined with dark, stubby lashes. "She died? I don't want you to die, Mom!" Under the restaurant's dim yellow lights, his skin was etched porcelain.

Stephanie rolled the tip of her cigarette in the ashtray until the cherry fell off and glowed among the ashes, getting more and more dim as it consumed itself and faded completely, only the thinning wisps of smoke above their heads mourning its departure. When she was certain the cigarette was no longer burning, she put it inside her pack, nestled in with the others, its butt slightly tar-stained.

"I'm going to have grilled cheese!" James announced his decision like a triumph, as if he had won the school spelling bee. "With French fries and Sprite, because I can't have Mr. Pibb after seven o'clock because it has too much caffeine. Right, Mom?"

After they ordered, Marla escaped to the salad bar, piling every vegetable except for lettuce onto her plate. Ray watched her careful, methodic motions as she moved from one taupe-colored container to another, until she reached the dressings, careful about her selection, and finally, two packages of oyster crackers, which she clutched in her hand as she marched back to the table.

The waitress gave them a cutting board with a small loaf of brown bread and a large serrated knife, a scoop of sweet-tasting butter slouching softly in a ramekin on the side.

Stephanie reached for the bread as Marla began to eat her salad, one vegetable at a time. She waved away Stephanie's bread offer, who buttered the piece and handed it to James.

"How is school going?" Ray asked, trying to establish a rhythm of conversation Marla could easily join.

"Good." James took another bite of his bread, smearing butter on the corner of his mouth. "Guess what we learned this week?" Ray scratched his red crayon across his placemat, covering all the white space with crimson wax.

"First, tell Marla what grade you're in." Ray touched James's hand, forcing him to surrender his crayon nub.

He looked at her. "Second," he said just before he shoved the last of his bread in his mouth. Marla nodded.

"What did you learn?"

"We learned all about Minnesota." James swung his feet back and forth, knocking his heals against the booth.

"Like what?"

James tilted his head to the side, pointed his chin at the ceiling, and tapped his finger against his jaw. "Like the state song, and the state bird, and the state flower, and the state fish. That kind of stuff."

Ray smiled, and to his surprise, Marla spoke up, her broccoli speared on the end of her fork, suspended halfway between her plate and her mouth. "I just learned the state's nickname on the way here." She popped the broccoli in her mouth and smiled as if she was creating suspense before revealing her secret.

"Actually, Minnesota has three nicknames."

Marla stared at James, forgetting about Ray and Stephanie. Ray watched her curiosity and suspicion at James's assertion. "Well, then I know one of them. The Land of 10,000 Lakes."

"Uh-huh," James said. "Everyone knows that one. It's on all the cars. But my teacher, Mr. Carlson, he said Minnesota actually has 12,000 lakes, but most people don't know that. It's also called the Gopher State, because we have Gophers here in the summertime, and what's the other one, Mom?"

Stephanie pointed her finger to the ceiling and winked at him.

"Oh, yeah," James said. "The North Star State. Because when you want to go north in Minnesota and you're driving and it's dark out, you can just follow the star. Mr. Carlson said in the olden days, people used to follow the star in their carriages and on their horses." James clapped his hands together once, proud of his lesson.

"Do you know what New Mexico is called?" Marla asked. "It only has one nickname."

James folded his arms on the table and leaned toward her. Ray watched, the two of them sharing the same fascination for useless facts. "What is it?"

"The Land of Enchantment. And the bird is the roadrunner, like the cartoon."

"Oh," James nodded, his thoughts serious and meditative. "I'm not allowed to watch that show."

When the waitress returned with Ray's credit card receipt, he scribbled a tip and signed it, without any offer from Stephanie to cover her part of the meal. Ray caught Marla trying to eye the total as he flipped the billfold shut and placed it at the edge of the table, and started to scoot out of the booth, James in tow.

"You want to sleep at the hotel, James?" Ray looked at him as his son sipped the rest of his Sprite through the plastic straw on his take-home kiddy cup.

James nodded. "I even brought my bathing suit so we can go swimming."

"His bag is in the car," Stephanie said as they approached the doors. "I have to get it out of the trunk."

Ray propelled Marla toward the rental car, his hand behind her by the elbow, trying to assess her mood. James ran up to them, and took the hand Ray was reaching toward Marla's, forcing her to pull away, James in between them, clutching his father's hand, and shoving the other one deep in his pocket, not looking at Marla. Ray thought of switching sides with Marla and taking her hand, but knew that no matter how he handled it, Marla had already noticed, had already been cast aside. The parking lot was dark, and Ray knew he would have to find his way back to the hotel, James in the backseat talking about school, Marla in the front seat, staring out the window. Ray looked up at the stars, but all he could see was Venus, a star in disguise, the rest blanketed by smog.

Honorable
Mention

But She Didn't Stay Long
Claudia Ivey

Remember a movie a while back where a young child was able to see dead people. Just by saying that, I realize many will know what movie I am talking about. I really didn't realize that I too had that gift, if you want to call it that... but since I usually don't pay attention on people's faces that much, I have no idea how many times that has actually happen to me. But there is one time, that I know for fact when I did.

This memory of that happened on a cold blizzardy day in the January of 2002. Normally on those kind of days I would hibernate at home and not even try to go out. But I had to go take my mom for a Radiation Treatment at the hospital. My mom was fighting Pancreatic Cancer, she had a big surgery, in the October before.

After that treatment, my mom wanted to go visit my Aunt. Now those road where all snowed covered, and that winds was so strong. Normally I would decline, but not today, I guess I wanted to please my mom. My aunt wasn't close by, a good ten or more miles away.

On our way, we decided it would best if we stopped and ate lunch, before arriving at my Aunt's.

If you know the Detroit Area, we were leaving Beaumont Hospital at Thirteen Mile Road, heading north on Woodward. There was a Beef Carver's Restaurant, just north of Square Lake Road on the East Side. That restaurant no longer stands there. Square Lake Road also known as Nineteen Mile Road.

I pulled up into the parking lot and headed for the open handicap spot in front of the restaurant's front doors. As I approach, I see that there is this old woman, whose view was first

---

hidden to me, by another parked van, is standing in front of that Handicap sign. I thought that she would move when she saw me entering that spot, but no, she just stood there. So I end up not pulling all the way up into that spot, like I was going to. I parked, and hurried out, to help my mom from the vehicle. But as I rush around the front of my car, I accidently bump into the woman's arm. I stopped quickly and turn around, saying "I'm sorry, I didn't mean to do that." while my mom is getting out and standing up. As I am talking to that lady, I stop, in my tracks, as I focus into her face. It isn't right. I put my hands on her shoulders, asking her "Are you OK???" The woman isn't looking at me, she is starring south east over my car, not once glancing elsewhere. I could see that this once well-dressed woman's clothes are now very aged, the white blouse, now yellow with a few moth holes in it, her leopard coat, also looked aged with moth holes, as well, was blowing wide open from the strong wind. She also had a hat on that matched up with her coat. But my eyes focus, I can see that her face, was off, not only was there eye makeup across and down her face, her lips are only held on her by thin lines of skin from under her nose. I could see her gums and teeth. I look back towards my mom, saying "Something is wrong." My mom then says, "Maybe she is waiting for someone."

I back up to continue towards helping my mom. As I take my mom into the restaurant, out of that frigid cold wind, that woman doesn't say anything or move. Now I don't know if you have any of the Beefcarver's chain around where you live, but it is set up like a cafeteria, you get in a line; pick up your food, pay, then servers take it to your table. I love their food and this was one of my mom's favorite places. This time when I went in, I got my mom in line, and went and got a server, letting them know that there is an old lady out in that cold, I think needed some help.

I watched through the block windows that are placed in the upper part of the double doors, that young male had to go through. I watch him go stand next to that lady right outside those doors, and he glanced around and hurried back in, out of that cold. Saying, "Sorry Ma'am, but I don't see no lady, she must of left." I didn't argue with him, I just was so surprise to hear him say that, after standing right next to her. My thoughts was "What? what do you mean, you didn't see her, are you kidding me." But I stayed quiet, I didn't want to sound crazy.

I turned to join my mom in line, and we got our food. We were seated next their nice warm fireplace, in front of the window, with my car and that woman right in my sights. I know my mom saw her, so I wasn't the only one. While I ate, I witness a couple more customers accidently hitting into her, I even saw her body react to those hits, as it swayed back and forth. But the difference was, no one stopped to look back at her to say they were sorry. And not once would she take her sights away from whatever she was looking at. The only thing my mom said about that woman, while eating that day, was repeating what she had said, when we were outside.

When I was almost done with my food, I saw a tall, thin, with a very dark skin complexion, in a white apron, white shirt, and white pants, and a chef hat, exit their kitchen through the double doors, that positioned behind the cashier, and he walked straight to me. I looked up at him, as he smiled and said. "Oh ma'am, don't worry about her, she comes here every so often, but she doesn't stay here long;" and turned around and walked right back to their kitchen. After I watch him walk out of my sight, I glance back outside, to look at that lady, but now she was gone. And I laughed, like that just didn't happen. I know my mom's reaction was like mine. I told my mom that I wanted to find out about more, that I will be right back. I was now just so curious, and happy to see someone else actually saw her, besides my mom & I. I got up and walked over to the cashier, asking "Could I please ask that cook, that just went back there something?" The employee asked me what this cooked looked like and I told her. Then she looked at me, saying "Sorry, ma'am, we don't have anyone that works here, with that description." Oh, my, I just couldn't believe that she just said that to me. That bothered me so so much. I went back to my table and told my mom what happened. Finished eating, and then we left. I will never forget that day.

Till this day, when I drive by that area, I glance that way, in hopes of seeing her, but never have since. I think that tall thin very dark skin black man, all in white, that came out to talk to me that day, was an angel.

Honorable
Mention

Copy
Claudia Ivey

Visiting some friends one day in a small campground, back in 1982, we came across a small white kitten, with two dark spots between her ears. This little fur ball had been shot by a Beebee gun. We checked around to see if anyone knew where she came from, but found no one. We end up taking that baby home. We got the bebe removed out of her and named her Xerox. Not long after taking Xerox in, we moved to another location, and ended up also adding a pup, who we name as Kemo. Both Kemo and Xerox become important part of my family, who is loved by all in our family.

We had moved to a two bedroom ranch type house, that has a breezeway between the house and garage, on seven acres. With our three children. I had lost my job, because of MS and was denied for disability and we had to downsize, where we lived.

One night, as my husband was sleeping in his chair, our children was asleep, I heard on the news about a black panther that was set free to roam in the area where we lived. The news warned us not to let any small pets out. Not long before I let my cat outside, she had grown before this incident happened. I got scared with what the news said and woke up my husband to see if he could get Xerox, back in the house. He went out in our back yard, it had just started raining, and started calling "Here Kitty, Kitty, Here Kitty, Kitty." in the darkness towards some bushes, when it hit him, that I had him yelling that with a big black cat out there. Boy did he come in quickly yelling at me, wanting to know if I had sent him out to be killed.

There were actually two panthers let loose, one in Michigan, close to the Ohio border, that was a declawed ninety pound female, and then the one in our area, had two inch claws, one sixty pound male. After that, Xerox became an indoor cat. And Kemo, wasn't let out, without us.

After that night Xerox was out, she had become a young expecting cat. She had her first and only litter of five in our breezeway. Four of those babies were black and white, but the last born was an all-white, long hair, little female, that we end up keeping, and we name her Copy.

What I loved about Xerox, that she had extra claws, and so did all five of those babies. The first born front paws was like he had double paws, per foot, he was such a doll too. He was the only male. One of the female's markings was like she was the opposite of a skunk, mostly white with the black stripes down the back, tail and up unto her head. We called her Flower.

It was hard on my five year old daughter, when those babies left to their new homes. My little girl loved those babies so, so much. Then all my girl's attention went to Copy. That baby was great for my girl, my daughter could dress that baby up and play house with her, and that baby would just sit her and let her do that.

When Copy was a year old, we moved her, along with Xerox and Kemo to the city. That panther never got caught that I know of. But I know that panther did kill a race horse that lived down the street from us. They all had run of our new house, but Xerox got ill, and lost most her fur, because of cancer and wound up losing her, about a year after we moved to the city.

Now I had no idea that when we named that kitten, Copy of ours, but that name so well suited her.

I am not sure how long we lived in our Jewell house, before we started having a different kind of experiences with our cat.

One day we were having a dear friend come visit, who we knew since our school days. This person lived on the other side of our state. We would have the pleasure of his attendance once or twice a year and he would always bring his dog.

Well Copy, didn't like any other animals visiting in her domain. She was just too eager to attack. So we would contain her in our basement, while that pup was there. One time I received a call, letting me know that he would be there shortly. I hung up my phone, and as I picked Copy up off our couch, talking to two of my children. We walked to the basement steps, and gently put her down and watch her scamper down the stairs. We turned around to exit the landing, shutting the basement door behind us. And we walked back to the living room, finding Copy laying on the couch, like we had never moved her. All of us was shocked, as we looked at her, there was no way she should be there, we just watched her go to the basement, there was no mistake. As we repeated that action, we all laughed, and watched Copy again run off, down those steps to the basement.

After that, as the years pass, we actually get to repeat that experience several times. Now we get to keep this kitty for a total of eighteen years. The older she got the less of that action we saw. Until we had an incident of another kind by my cat.

Over those later years, my son had moved out. We take in another person, who came with her own cat, Julian, and my oldest took on another cat, named Luxly, that she was watching for a friend of hers. Those two cats, a male and a female, stayed up on the second floor and they got along well together.

One, nice sunny day, I was sitting on my couch, in my living room, with my feet up, reading my laptop. This time it was Copy that was curled up next to me sleeping. In the distance, I can hear the girl's upstairs, talking and laughing... My oldest daughter, her friend, and another visitor.

All of a sudden I hear a very loud cat fight echo throughout my house. Copy sits up, hurries off my couch, and runs towards the front door, as I hear someone races down the steps from the second floor. It was the person that has moved in with us, she runs into the living room, she's my cat next to the front door, and runs over grabbing Copy and started hitting on her.

I yelled "Stop hitting my cat!!!! Put her down!!" Then I get told "Copy, just attacked my cat!!!" And I then said "What, Copy has been laying down next to me the full time." The young woman, looks at me, and quickly sets Copy back down and runs back up stairs.

A few minutes later, my daughter comes down stairs and tells me, "Mom, while we were talking, Copy came in my room; attacking... she jumped on Julian and through her on her back, pinning her down by her throat. Then she got chased down the steps, after Copy was spotted in the living room, you said that Copy had been there the whole time. Was Copy really with you?"

"Yeah, Copy was sleeping next to me; sleeping on the couch... I could hear that cat fight." We figured that had to be Copy's double.

Another time after that, my oldest went up to her room, and when she opened her bedroom door, she saw Copy in there, hissing at the other two cats, she grabbed Copy and when she opened the door to put Copy out, Copy still in her hands, she sees the other Copy on the floor looking up at her. Not knowing what to do, she put the Copy that she was holding down, and closed her bedroom door quickly, and stayed in there for a good while.

Not long after that, Copy gets an infected tooth, her little cheek swells up and I took her to the vet. Copy ended up getting three teeth pulled, but while our old cat was under, she had a stroke. We brought her home and she passes on a few days later on that March day in 2001. I loved that cat, and she will always have a place in my heart.

****

One summer day that year, I was in the basement sitting on the steps, waiting for the dryer to stop, it had a very small load to dry.. My oldest came and joined me, as we started talking about the plans we had for that day. We were laughing when we both saw something move. We looked towards the movement, and both saw Copy, coming out of the darkness, while she around the our large octopus type furnace. Not a word came out of either of us. When Copy got in front of us, she stopped and looked up at us, and then cut across to the other side of the steps. We both stood up to see where she was going, but now she was out of sight. We both couldn't believe that we got to see our Copy one more time. That was the last time I got to see my cat.

Eighth Month Party
Carol Hanson

It was eighth month party day. A perfect day filled with the promise of sunshine and wispy clouds on a back lit azure sky to put a close to our summer parties. A definite making Michigan memories kind of day.   My grandparents knew how to make any day just a little bit more fun by putting titles on these events. The eighth month party signified that summer was winding down, and everyone would soon be going their own way as the school year approached.

I had loved these parties for as long as I could remember, but in the summer they got bigger and better. My grandparents both came from a family of seven, and summer was the optimal time for those who couldn't get here during the rest of the year to visit. I knew who my aunts, uncles and first cousins were, but when family from out of state would visit, I would just give them the same title to keep it less confusing. Each get together would include an 8" x 10" glossy photo of us as a group, thanks to one of the uncles being a photographer.

My grandparent's house was not large, but the acreage they had was. My grandpa built a huge barbecue pit, and in the summer there was always a slathering of ribs cooking on the pit. Those smells just wafted up like a balloon releasing from a child's hand.

The party was never complete without watermelon, and of course, a seed spitting contest. I loved that mouthwatering watermelon, and the gushing sound it made when the knife was rushing through it. I remember when I was four I had a dress that my Uncle Danny called my watermelon dress. It was green and white striped like the rind of a melon. I always recalled that whenever we had watermelon.

From a young age I had started keeping a diary, but for special occasions I wrote a journal and would draw a few crude pictures. At our next family event, I would share my entries with everyone in attendance. Of course, no one always remembered something happening the way I wrote it, but then they couldn't dispute it either. Over the years, I would see the entries get longer and the pictures actually look better. Family members would say I had a knack for drawing. That much they all agreed on.

Our 8th month party always took place at Bushman Lake in Clifton Mills, which was privately owned by family members. My great-great grandparents had settled there when Michigan was still a territory. Although we went there a lot during the summer, and for ice skating in the winter, I always seemed to love it best for the 8th month party.

I can still see those red and white gingham oil cloths that we would adorn the picnic tables with. If the wind caught them just right, they looked like flower petals blowing in the wind. The food that was laid on these tables left hardly a speck of the oil cloth underneath.

The men would spend most of the day on the lake in row boats hoping to bring back the one "that didn't get away." They actually made it a contest. Each would put in a dollar or two, and the pot would go to the owner of the biggest fish. That lake had spawned some of the best fish around; largemouth bass, northern pike, and pumpkin seed sunfish to name a few. When the catch was brought in for the day, the women had to do the measuring because the men just couldn't agree on what constituted the largest.

My cousins spent most of the day in the water or playing badminton or croquet on the uneven and lumpy grass. The afternoon was winding down, and a few family members had left the beach for the day. I had my sketch pad and had been drawing throughout the day. I usually photographed what I was going to draw with my Polaroid OneStep, so I could instantly see what my subject was if I needed to make subtle changes.

My last picture was of my two year old cousin Sally. I had turned fourteen that summer, and Sally was the youngest and most adored cousin of mine. She had these strawberry blond curls that just seemed to go on forever and like my grandmother would say she was "as cute as a button."

I had been babysitting Sally for over a year now, and it was the best fifty cents an hour I ever made. She loved it when I sang "Lollipop" to her. When I made the popping sound with my cheek, she would giggle, clap her hands, and say "again". She would try to mimic the sound, but it ended up sounding more like the "raspberries" I would blow on her stomach.

Sally sat pretty still for a long time playing in the sand without realizing that I was drawing her likeness. Besides the curls, she had these blue eyes that were the same color of the delphiniums in our summer garden. Her still baby fat arms were just giving that sand a good working over. Her laughter filled the air, and brought a smile to my face. It resonated like an echo coming off a canyon wall. Soon enough my Aunt Mattie came and scooped Sally up to put her down for a nap. I popped my cheek for Sally, as her head hit my aunt's neck. As she was leaving, my aunt turned around and gave me a wink and I returned it. This was something that my aunt and I had done for as long as I could remember.

Sally was taking a nap in the family station wagon when terror struck. The vehicle that she was napping in was atop a hill. Somehow without the will of nature or provocation, the car began careening down the hill and into the lake. My aunts and cousins all ran toward the vehicle screaming and trying to get the attention of the men in the boats.

At that point, everything seems to move in slow motion. Things that were so clear just moments earlier, now took on a hazy state. I threw down my art supplies and raced into the water with the others. Everyone seemed to be in a state of confusion and shock. The windows that had been open a crack had taken on water. The doors would not budge.

My uncles finally saw us flailing about moving frantically in the water. It was their hardest row ever. The gap between them and us seemed immeasurable, as if they were weighted down by anchors. When the men finally reached the site, they descended as the army had done at Normandy. They realized what was happening and took their oars and furiously tried to break the windows. When the glass in the back window finally gave up its battle, so had Sally.

There was nothing more that could be done. All efforts to revive her were futile. She had drowned during this freak and unexplainable event. The grownups tried to shield us kids from what was unfolding before our eyes, however, the last thing I saw were Sally's strawberry blond curls which were now mashed to her face, being placed under a blanket. My heart felt as if stones from the water had been lodged in it.

As it turned out, this would be our last eighth month party. August would come around again, but the haunting of Sally's tragic death would stay with us forever and overshadow what should have been a perfect summer day.

Jewel House
Claudia Ivey

When something out of the normal happens, it is always good to experience it with another person, so you don't think something is wrong with yourself. Because some of the memories alone, could've landed me hospitalized.

Back in 1984 my family moved back to the city, where my husband and I were raised. We had found an old house that was placed in a different corner of that suburb, that was affordable to us to buy. It was in September of that year when we moved in with our three children, our dog, Kemo, 1982-1992 (a shepherd/husky mix) and a cat, named Copy, 1982-2000. In this dwelling we live for the next twenty years. We moved to be able to be closer to our parents, to help them, as they aged.   My mother-in-law had already passed away, and his father was in need.

We moved from seven acres to a small lot.

We had no idea that we had moved into what one may call, a haunted house. And over the years that we lived there, we shared a lot of different experience. I know now that some people wouldn't had stayed there. But to me, it was safer inside, in that neighborhood, then out.

At first I didn't realize, it took a year or so before I even knew that this house was special. I guess I was just too busy to notice. I wasn't one to be even looking for that kind of activity. At this time in my life, I don't know if I even thought that kind of activity was really real or not. I know I saw that in movies, and what I had experiences, before then, I thought was probably some kind of prank to scare people. I had no inner proof, I guess that made me truly open my eyes. Until I moved into that neighborhood.

Now living in an active house, strange stuff surely didn't happen on a daily basis, but every once in a while, and it usually did it, when unexpected. So if I tried looking for it, I didn't see anything.

But over a twenty year period, we sure did collect a number of odd memories, and I want to share some of them with you.

Now I don't believe everyone can see or feel such activity, like they are blind to it or something, like my husband. Because he truly didn't experience stuff like the rest of his family did, while living there. He told me that there has been times in the basement he felt like he was being watched, but no one was there, and that didn't bother him. When we told him stuff, it was like he wasn't listening to us, that he didn't care, or that it was our problems or something. So it got to the point, why even say anything to him, he wasn't there for us on that kind of stuff.

Shortly after moving there, I learnt that one of my school friend's grandmother lived across the street. So this friend remembered some things about my house. One that stood out was about a young boy, around twelve, in the early 1960's, he aimed a gun at a target, he made on the basement wall, pulled the trigger, that bounces off that wall accidently killing himself.

Around 1986, in that large rectangle shaped living room, our couch was mainly placed on the south wall, facing north, towards the front windows, and our TV stand. The couch was longer than the wall there, and would stick up in the archway to our dining room. There would be times when I was watching TV, that I would see movement behind me, and out the side of my eyes, I could see a young boy standing behind me, watching the TV. But if I turned around to look towards our dining room, he would disappear. He never did anything wrong, and after I realized what was going on, I would try to look at him. But sometimes I would automatically turn my head, thinking that was my son there. This would only happen every so often. So I would get upset with myself, because I wanted to see him.

I never trained Kemo to really sit up or anything, but for some odd reason, he would do so, in the east/south corner of our living room, that was just so funny.

One night, my son woke up to a burning smell, and when he opened his eyes, there was a man standing at the foot of his bed, he looked up at this man, and the man said "Go back to sleep, your sister burnt the cookies, she's making." Normally my son would of ran out of there, but he even surprised himself, he couldn't believe that he rolled over and went back to sleep. He didn't know if he dreamt that or not, it just felt so real. He asked his oldest sister if she made any cookies during the night, and she said No, but there was many times she would do that.

One night, around midnight, she was making cookies, I was still up, and was standing in the kitchen talking to her. When both of us heard a loud wind type noise, I turned around and listened to the refrig, but nooo, the noise was coming pass that. The doorway to the basement and back door is next to the refrig... both my daughter and I walk over to the basement landing and listened and that wind noised, turned into distorted mumbling and laughter, like that was a loud party going on in the basement. We looked at each other, and rushed away from that area, closing the door, to that area. My girl hurries and turns off the oven, and we hurry off to bed, leaving the cookies alone, till morning. The next day we laughed about that.   We heard that sound from the basement a couple of times, after that night. We can't understand a word that was said, but we know laughing when we hear it.

In 1987, my father in law passes away, we wanted to move into his big house. But it took too long to sell. Well we cleaned our house up really nice, to show. One day, while my children was at school, and my husband was at work. I went to go wash a few dishes, but as I went to grab the dish soap, it disappears in front of me. I thought, boy am I tired, I swear it was there. So I ran down to the basement to see if it was near the wash tub, after not finding that soap wasn't anywhere in the kitchen. After checking the bathroom on the main floor and not finding it there, I ran up to the 2nd floor checking the bathroom up there. No luck. I came back downstairs, and my son comes in from school, and as he starts to head for his room, I asked him…" "Do you know where the dish soap is?" And he said "No" as he comes to a dead stop on the steps, and then says "Come here Mom. I turned and went up the few steps, and through our metal railing we have around this stairway, I see my dish soap, in the middle of my floor, with a bunch of my daughter's toys circling it. Now I just walked through there, and it was totally clear. I laughed; I couldn't believe that just happened. My son runs up the steps and hands me that soap, and I have him put his sister's toys back away. To me that was funny.

As my children grew up, there was times they would want some of their friends to stay over for the night. I didn't care, it was ok for me. But then it ended up that something scared them and they would want to go home during the middle of the night, crying, I would have to take them home. A few refused to stay over after that.

I know I feared a black shadow type outline of a man that we would see in there, and my son had a problem with some old man, that once chased him through my house, as two of his friend watched through our living room windows.

My son first saw that old man, while doing dishes. That man was looking at him through our kitchen window, standing in our back yard. My son yelled, running out of the kitchen, and my husband went in the back to go after him, but no one was there.

Next time, my son and daughters saw the old man looking in an upstairs window, and again, my husband run's to go after that man, but no one was there. And the next time my kids saw that man in our backyard, from a upstairs window, they yelled. I was on our front porch talking to a neighbor, I looked towards the back of our house, from our porch, and I saw that old man, he gave me the dirtiest look, before turning and walking through our privacy fence, that led to our next door neighbor. Then my husband yells, he just got out to the back yard, I yelled back saying the man headed west into the neighbor's yard. The neighbor that was on my porch with me, saw him too, and said "Did he just go through that fence?" My husband ran around to the front of the house. A neighbor from across the street, joined my husband in the search, but they found, no one.

Shortly after school started in 1989, my husband & I took our oldest shopping for a bathing suit, for swim class. My youngest was over at my parents, and my son was supposed to stay at a friend's house, till we got back. But no, while we were gone, my son took his friend over to our house to get a toy. His friend stayed on the front porch, as one of my oldest daughter's friend joined him on the porch. When my son came back down from his room with toy in hand, he encounters that old man. Now the two on the porch is watching this through our living room window. They can see the old man blocking my son's way. My son darted to his left out of the dining room, into my bedroom, closing the door, behind him. But that old man walks through that solid door, going after my son. My son gets on the other side of my bed, grabbing the phone.

My son calls my dad. Now my dad in the May before had a five bypass open heart surgery. My son is yelling that there is a man after him, and that he's scared, and hiding under my bed. My parents rush into the car, with my youngest and rushes over to my house. When they turn on to our street he see two kids jumping up and down in the middle of the street yelling and pointing. With a baseball bat, my dad goes into the house, to protect my son. The old man disappears. My dad doesn't find anyone, and as he is bringing my son out of the house, we were arriving home. We got to hear the excited kids telling their story. I was so worried about my dad. This is in 1989, before I had a cell phone, but I now wish I had back then.

After losing Kemo, our dog, in 1992, we get a wolf hybrid, named Moke... We have only one story to share with Moke... One time after seeing the shadow man, while trying to do my laundry in the basement. I went running to get out of that area, fearing that he was following me. My youngest wanted to know what I saw her, while now standing in the living room. This daughter, never seen that dark figure before, darted towards the kitchen wanting to see this. Moke, ran after her, which this is the only time in his life time that he did this, he grabs her, by the back of the shirt, to pull her back in the living room. Oh yes, Moke was afraid of our basement. There are times when he was in the backyard, he would bark to come in. Most time he had no problem -coming in, when I would open the door, but there was times, where he would rush backwards off the back porch, crying... and then we would have to go down the steps and pick that ninety pound dog up and bring him into the house. He would fight us, till we got past those basement steps, into the kitchen and shut that basement door. We had Moke from 1992 to 2002, he dies of cancer. In 1997 we got a second dog, as a pup. The people across the street from me that I babysat forgot pups, and we got one. His name was Toby, his mom was an American Eskimo and dad was a championship Sheltie, Toby looked like Sheltie. We had Toby from 1997 to 2013. My mom took one of their pups too... sassy. 1997-2012.

After that, I hired a man to come in to try to get rid of that man. He was scaring my son too much. It cost me $150. He told me that there was many souls in our house with two doorways that he couldn't close. He said he got rid of the old man, after we heard him have a big fight upstairs in my son's room. And told us that he sent that black shadow guy away, but he was afraid that one would come back, because he couldn't close that door. The black shadow guy didn't show up again for a couple of years.

One time in 1996, my oldest invited a friend, that she met over the internet, from Canada, when she arrived at the door, she backed up, insisting to be taken to a motel, said that she was sorry, she can't come in. She had come here to go to a concert, with my daughter. While out with my girl, she told my daughter that she saw something evil, in my house that scared her. This girl had no idea that it was haunted, after all we didn't tell everyone; it wasn't on our mind all the time.

Shortly after I started getting on the internet, I got a laptop in 1998. I found out that people were recording ghost voices and sounds, so I went out and bought some tape for my recorder and

I actually recorded some voices in our basement. I learnt a big lesson, though, never use the same tape, the next night, I tried it again, and the tape was totally destroyed along with the recorder. My husband had mention, maybe set up his video recorder camera, and glad he didn't do that. The recording I did get, was at the end of the tape, it was mostly static, then it sounded like my husband's chair being dragged, and then papers being gone through, then real soft, had to listen When softly, but we heard music, like some kind of Indian music....then heard some guys talking but couldn't understand them and either two lambs or goats baaing. That hit me funning. Couldn't understand what those guys were saying though.

When I first got my laptop, I already knew how to email my friends, but I saw my girls were chatting with people, and I wanted to learn how to do that. My oldest put me in a chat room, about ghost. I watched a little bit, what people were talking about, before adding anything. A woman started asking me questions and I let her about my house.

Then out of the blue, this woman asked if she could come over... surprised, I said "Okay, where are you at??" she said "New York." I asked her if when, she wanted to do this, and she said right now. What, right now, I thought, how can she do this... then she asked if she could bring her friend that lives in Indiana, and I am in Michigan. Now I wanted to see what they were talking about, and said ok. Then she told me, not to tell me anything. This woman impressed me, as she says she enters my house, she describes it to a tee. Even told me where my husband was. She lets me know about some woman in my kitchen that was upset, because she was upset, because she was left handed and felt like I was only buying utensils for the right handed, she had me yell in the kitchen letting her know that they could be used with either hand, and I did. She let me know that there was many souls in this house, and one was a sobbing woman sitting on my basement steps. She saw a young man with a mean looking dog on my steps going upstairs. And that there is a family dog of ours that is a protector that would've been Kemo. I know one morning when my youngest woke up, she saw Kemo laying his head on her bed, and she was petting him. She then clothed her eyes, when she remembered that our Kemo had died, she reopens her eyes, and now Kemo is gone. So I knew Kemo was there. That was mostly what I remembered of that conversation went. Oh she had my daughter put us in some private chat room somehow, before going over this.

A couple of nights later, I was sitting on my couch, and my oldest daughter with a friend, was at our desk top, and all of a sudden, our new refrig, open and slammed shut, three times. No one was in the kitchen at that time. I was talking to that woman in that chat room at that time, and she said that lady in my kitchen was telling me Thank you. Now my girl knew about that lady in what she said a few nights before, and I let my daughter know what that lady said about why the refrig, and we all laughed.

One of my best examples of an experience is this one. One evening in the late 1990's, I was sitting on my couch, facing North, with my laptop in my lap, and our dog, Toby, asleep next to me. My oldest daughter, at our desktop, that was placed on a desk, on the far east wall. A popular talk show host was on our TV on the North wall, next to a black bird cage that our parrot, a blue and gold macaw, named Mickie, was sleeping in, on her swing. It was late, my husband already had gone to bed, and so was everyone else, in the house.

I wasn't paying too much attention to that talk show, I was more into talking to my friends, on my laptop, when all of a sudden, out of nowhere, there was like a big invisible dog fight, in front of me. My feet were up on the foot part of our reclining couch. I heard the growling, the sounds of teeth, as they were snapping at each other. I felt the vibration as they hit our hardwood floor, and hit against the foot of my couch, that my feet were up on. I freeze in my spot, afraid to move. My dog, Toby wakes up, startled and jumps off of the couch, biting up at the air, as he joins into the fight. Our parrot, Mickie, falls off her swing, to the floor of her large cage, with her wings spread out, as she tries to flatten herself, as close to the ground as she can, to protect herself. My daughter also freezes over at the desktop. That loud dog fight, only lasts, I don't even think for one minute, but it felt like forever. And as fast as it came, it was totally gone. I ached after words, like I got hit by a car or something.   After that attack clears away, Toby stops, and glances around before jumping back up onto the couch. Toby lies back down, still showing his teeth, towards the floor. Micky stays still until Toby stops showing his teeth, as he starts playing with a toy of his that was on the couch prior to the attack. Micky finally climbs back up on the side of her cage, back to her swing, all fluffed up. Then my daughter says "Now mom, tell me that you just heard that." I laughed and said "Yes, now it is time for me to go to bed..."

"Mom, wait for me, don't leave me in here alone." my daughter says, as we quickly shut down our computers, and turn off the TV and lights. My room was my safe point. My girl runs back to her room, where she felt better too.

In 2001, I went to stay with my mom, when she got cancer. When she was doing better, I was able to leave her alone for a bit, as I did some chores, like paying bills, and cleaning our parrot's cage. One day, before running to pay the bills, I stopped by my house that was about a mile south of my mom's, I went there to see if my daughters wanted to go with me. Both my girls existed the house, and as one gets in my car to come with me, the other goes over to the driver's side, in our driveway. to let me know that she is working, and couldn't come, but wanted me to come back to get her, if we decided to go out to eat. As I went to say, my girl yells, as she darts back at the house. I turn to see what is going on, as my youngest jumps out of the car to follow her sister. I yell "What's wrong??" and my youngest answers as she runs to the house, There is a man in the house." I quickly look up towards my daughter's bedroom windows that face the front of the house, in time to see the curtain fall back into place. I get out to go in, I have MS, and it takes me a lot longer to get from one place to another. By time I get into our living room, my girls are coming back down stairs, and as I walk towards them, as they enter the living room, from our dining room, our parrot says "Well, did you find anyone?" startled we all look at our bird as my youngest answered "No".

We never heard Micky talk that well before. She would say things, like Hello, and stuff like that, and one other time our parrot made us laugh, after she laid her first egg. It had dropped to the floor of the cage, January 1996, we got her from my cousin in Oct 1995, and she was ten years old. When the egg dropped, my youngest and I were in the living room. I walked over, opened her cage, picked up the egg in my opened hand and put it up in front of our bird, and I said "Good girl, good girl," and then the bird looked at the egg real close, with a tilted head and then lifted up her head and said "It's a Girl!!" both my daughter and I laughed, we thought that was so funny.

But after she said, "Well, did you find anyone?" Those were her last words, because she was found dead in her cage the next morning. I know she had gotten scared in that house a few times, and her cage needed to be covered at night. I don't know if she was covered up the night before or not. My daughter told me that she was fine the evening before, because she had Micky out playing with her. We all miss that beautiful bird very much. But that was the worst thing that happened in our house while we were there. When my daughter had run up in her room, there was no one there, but a bunch of old stuff like watches and jewelry that we never saw before, on her bed, that was next to her bedroom windows, that face the front of our house.

When we were selling that house, we had a couple of ghost groups go through that house, they did record some voices.

My best friend told me after I sold that house that she was scared of my house... she would never come over to come in to visit, we would always go out. The first ghost group that came over, equipment wouldn't work on the main floor.

After we sold that house, the new owner rents it out, about five years later; one of my son's old school friends sees him on the computer and lets my son know that he is now renting our old house. My son gets invited over. This guy wanted to know if we had anything odd going on in this house. My son told him about some of the incidents we had. Well this guy's girlfriend, got all scratched up and pushed down the steps, getting her to leave him. And that he has been having big problems. Not long after that, the friend moves out of that house. That is the only time I heard on that house.

I do miss that house; it had a nice big living room. My husband fixed it up really nice before selling it; I wished it looked like that when we lived there. We didn't care that it was haunted, in fact it let us share some odd memories... yeah there was time it did get to me... the worse, was losing our parrot, Micky. The only other time while we got hurt from something odd in that house.

My oldest was in her room, when she witness one of her souvenir glasses, raised up off her dresser, floated half way across the room, before falling, smashing against her hardwood floor, and she caught a small piece of glass in her face.

Memories of a
Paranormal Kind
Claudia Ivey

The story I am about to share with you, is something that I witnessed some years ago. This is a true story. Only I have changed the names to protect the people who are involved in this pass memory of mine.

First I need to let you know some history before I get into this fantastic memory I want to share. Back in 1984, my husband & I bought a house that sits just North of Detroit, in a suburb. We moved into a dwelling that is seated one house from the corner, off a main road. But this story isn't about my family, but about the house across the street.

There was a senior citizen that lived there alone. I befriend this very active individual. And over time I was educated about her family and we shared many laughs together. I am going to call her Eve, she moved there back in the 1930's. She had her family there, four children, three girls and a boy. She lost her husband early on. She put a lot of hard work into that house, including having a basement added.

She only gets to raise three of those four children. The youngest, who I call Jessica, dies at the age of four years old, from high fevers, in that house. Her ashes were placed in an urn that was kept in the linen closet, in the hallway, by the bedrooms and bathroom on the main floor.

Now this is ghost story, but don't worry, it's not a scary scenario, but one from a child's eyes, that I feel is needed to be heard.

I loved visiting Eve, and over the years we became very good friends. At first when I met her, she loved working in her garden, she belong to a bowling league, with a group of her friends. She loved sharing her stories with me when she was young. One of my favorites that she shared was that she was raised in Ohio and would ride her pony to her one room school house. As time went by, I noticed that she was having a harder time getting around. I got to know her now adult children. One daughter, lived about 5 miles away, another was a good 10 miles or more away, and her son, lived on the East Coast. They were happy that I lived across the way of their mother, earning their trust, they shared their phone numbers in case I ever needed to call them. Many times when I made my dinner for my family, I would take a dish over for Eve, making sure that she was getting enough to eat.

One year, Eve's son was visiting his mom, during the Christmas Holidays. I was so happy he was there. It was between Christmas and New Year's. Eve has a stroke; it was early in the evening. A lot of the neighbors came out, as they watched her being taken away in an ambulance. Including my neighbor's son who has is known for breaking into homes. Eve's son also went to the hospital, with his mom.

The next day, I was working in my house when a neighbor that lives a door away from me, knocks on my door. He wanted to let me know that he spotted Eve's back door was left open. Eve's property is border with an alley that separates her land from the business that faces the main road. Many of us neighbors would walk through that alley to go to a party store that was on the next block. There was a fresh snow that night before. I walked over with my neighbor to see what he had spotted. Sure enough the door was open; we also spotted tracks in the new snow, which led from the alley to that back door. We walk to the front of the house and notice those tracks lead right over to my neighbor's house, from Eve's front door. I call Eve's daughter to inform her what I have learned and called the police.

Sure enough, Eve's house was broken into. The only thing that was missing Eve's family knew of was a gift she received that Christmas, a VCR, still in its box. She never had a VCR before. Her children didn't care that was gone, but was bothered big time, that someone broke into her home. The intruder didn't just steal, but he also trashed Eve's home. Including breaking the urn that she thought was in a safe place. I know, I was the one that had to try to clean this up. The ashes were dumped out all over a hardwood floor, and I couldn't get all them up out of the cracks. That urn was totally smashed beyond repair...

That thief was never caught, even though I showed that tracks in the snow to the police, with them saying that it wasn't enough evidence.

After that, Eve never returns to her beloved home, that she treasures. Her descendants don't trust her living there alone anymore. Eve moves to a senior citizen apartments, nearby. Her family sells her home.

A young family moves in. They have two daughters, one is eightenn months old and the other is three and a half. Both parents work.

Eve resides at that senior apartments for a few months. I would go visit her, she liked it, but she missed her place. One day I called Eve up on the phone and the conversation went like this:

Me: "Hi Eve"

Eve: "Who is this?" and I told her my name.

Eve then said "Oh, it was so nice talking to you and that we got to do this again sometime." and she hung up.

I immediately called her daughter that lived nearby, to go check on her mom. Sure enough, Eve who is now in her mid-80's and needed attention. They move Eve to the younger daughter's home, which lived farther away. This cuts out my visits, but would get to see her only a few times after that. Her son would bring her over to drive by, so she could see her house. But she didn't know the people that moved in her place.

Meanwhile, we have this new family now living in Eve's home. Over the next couple of years, they become my friends. I am going to call them Mike & Tina, and their daughters Lacy (the oldest) and Tammy.

When Tammy became of age to be able to start Kindergarten, Mike and Tina needed a babysitter. I volunteered to take on that task. Both daughters were a pleasure to take care of. Tammy went to Kindergarten in the mornings, and Lacy was now in 2nd grade. I would arrive early, and get the girls ready for school and take them. I would then go pick up Tammy at noon, and stay with her, then pick up Lacy when she got out of school and stay with them till about 6pm.

After sitting for a short time, I noticed Tina looking ill, darkness under her eyes, just overly tired. I asked Tina, if she was doing ok. She informed me that Tammy was keeping her up most of the night. The trouble with Tammy would start at bedtime; she would start crying and having big fits, not wanting to go down when it was time. All Tammy would say that was too scared, but not why. Tina would end up taking that little one in her room to sleep, and Tammy would keep Tina up, because she was so restless throughout the night. Tina asked me, knowing that Tammy liked talking to me, if I could find out what was going on. I told Tina, that I would see what I could find out.

The next day, when I picked up Tammy from kindergarten, I brought her home, and gave her lunch. Then afterwards, while watching one of her favorite shows, I asked Tammy, why she was having such a hard time going to bed for her mommy. Tammy told me because she was scared at night... I then asked her "Of what?" And then she said that there was this little girl in her room every night.

"What??? A little girl... Oh Tammy, you don't need to be scared of her, that is just Jessica... she was a good little girl, that is Eve's little girl...They use to live here, and Jessica got real sick and her mommy couldn't save her... she is just seeing you as another little girl... all you have to do is smile and wave at her, and she should go away." Tammy was so happy I told her this and gave me a hug.   A couple of days later, Tammy came running to me after school, saying that I was right. Jessica would wave back to her and then go away. At the end of the week, I see Tina for the first time, since I talked to Tammy, Mike has been getting home first. She asked me what I told her daughter. Now that scared me, I had no idea how she was going to react. I asked her, if she was still having that problem, and she said "No, now Tammy is begging to go to bed at night.

I told Tina, that outside her daughter's room, that an urn had broken the ashes of the previous owner that was still in that hardwood floor. I told Tina that Tammy said that she was seeing a little girl, and I let Tammy know that Jessica was a good little girl, that she just wants to say Hi.

Tina, said that worked, and she was getting the rest she needed.

Over the next couple of years, I would hear every once in a while from Tammy. "I got to see Jessica last night." and smiles.

One Sunday night, I got a call from Eve's youngest daughter; she let me know that her mother had passed on.   I felt so bad.

Now my neighbor's that lives in Eve's home, don't know Eve. At this time, I no longer sit for the girl's in the mornings; their daddy takes them to school. Tammy is now in 2nd grade, it is spring time. That Monday, when I went to go pick up the girl's from school, Tammy was the first little one out of that building that day. Normally those two would be the last ones existing that place. She came racing across that playground, jumping into my car, yelling "I got some news" I told her "So do I, but I rather hear your news, first." Tammy then told me "I am not going to see Jessica anymore, because her mommy came and got her last night." Then Tammy got real sad "I am going to miss my friend" but she then added that she was happy that her mommy came and got her. I was just floor, her family had no idea that Eve had passed away. Even though I told Tammy about Jessica, it really didn't validate in my mind that she was really seeing Jessica, until she said that. I was so happy to hear that Eve came and got her little girl. I had to tell Eve's daughters about that event, and it brought tears to their eyes. I don't think I will ever forget about that experience that child had, that I got to share, thank you, Tammy!!!

Newly Made Farm Girl
Elizabeth Farney Maxson

I grew up in beautiful Dayton, Ohio. A city known for Wright Patt Air Force Base's controversial involvement with Area 51, the birthplace of aviation, and of course the University of Dayton. In fact, I grew up less than three miles from UD's campus and less than a block away from a local city park. I played basketball, baseball, and tennis at the park every summer, trick-or-treated with my pillow case to the local pizza places for free food every Halloween, and rode my bike everywhere.

So, when I announced that I was accepting a job an hour north in the heart of Shelby County, my parents laughed. The idea of me living deep in farm country offered amusement for almost everyone in my family. Ironically, my dad's mom moved to Dayton from the town I was moving to and both of my mom's parents moved to Dayton from the back hills of Tennessee. So why was it so funny for me to be making this country move? Well, I was never what you might call "the really outdoorsy type." Camping meant Girl Scouts, latrines, and weekends only. Also, my brother has always been allergic to well... everything and I was never a kid who liked to get really dirty. We had pets: a parakeet that flew into a wall, hamsters that killed each other, and fish that all inevitably took the almighty water journey to the sea. So, this move would be quite a change, but I thought I was ready. Moreover, I was in love and ready for a new life, new people, and new challenges. Look out Mary Tyler Moore! I was making the city to country switch and nothing was going to hold me back...

The first morning on the farm was great. I felt the sunshine in every pore of my body. I soaked in the smells, fed the dogs, and I felt like I was going to burst into song every second. I looked around and saw nothing but happiness. My husband was off working on a movie set in Pennsylvania. So here I was, less than a month into my transition to the green acres of Ohio among fields of soybeans, corn, and wheat, and he left me with a farm to take care of. I had my boots on, jeans ready, and I walked out to the barn confident and exuberant.

This would be a good time to mention that I had been left basically two major duties to attend to while my husband was away. I had to take care of the baby chicks and our three energetic dogs. It was spring, so these chicks were little. They had been mailed to the local post office and after they were picked up, brooders were set up to keep them warm, confined, and safe. I can't even express the surprise on my face when we walked into the post office, heard all of the chirping, and walked out with all of the chicks. After they were settled, my only real concern was not the one hundred baby chickens that were going to be in my sole care, but the likelihood that I might lose some of them during my tenure as their protector and provider. My husband laughed at my distress and said not to worry. I would probably lose a few, but as long as I fed them and made sure they had clean water, most would survive until his return. I could live with a few dead chickens, considering there were a hundred of them and mom and I argued about how many "a few" were when I was nine. I was prepared to say goodbye to maybe three or four chicks.

So let's now rejoin me as I continued my joyful walk to the barn. I opened the old wooden door and made my way through the old milking barn to where the first of the three large brooders were set up. I lifted the lid and terror struck me. There were three dead chicks in the middle of the group. They were just lying there and the other chickens were walking on top of them like feathered doormats. I swallowed hard and closed the lid.

What do I do with dead chickens? I thought to myself. I hadn't asked that question, so I immediately pulled my cell phone out of my back pocket and called Pennsylvania. Voicemail. I left a message about the dead chicks and went back to the house to retrieve a plastic Wal-Mart bag to hold the dead chicks until I got further information. I started back out to the barn and nearly tripped over Andie. Andromeda, the smiling dog, jumped about my feet waiting for me to finish my chore so we could head out on our daily walk to the creek. I laughed and watched as she stayed outside the barn. She hated the barn and would always wait for me every time I entered.

I got back to the brooder, lifted the lid, and put on the rubber gloves I also got from the closet with the Wal-Mart bag. If I had to touch dead baby chicks, I certainly wasn't going to get my hands grossed up. I dropped the three dead chicks into the bag, fed and watered the still living chicks, and closed the lid. I moved to the medium brooder and opened it. There were two more dead chicks in this one! I could feel the tears starting to well up, but I blinked them back, dropped them both into the bag, fed and watered the live chicks, and closed the lid. The last brooder offered a bit of a reprieve. There was only one dead chick and there was plenty of water so all I needed to do was remove the dead one and add feed.

I walked out of the barn feeling semi-nauseous and dropped the bag onto the ground. I removed my gloves and again pulled out my cell phone only to hear my husband's voice telling me leave a message at the beep.

"What do I do with dead baby chickens? Byeeeee." It was a pleasant enough message, but I felt extremely foolish for having to call him the first morning of my solo farm experience. After ten minutes, I walked over to the plastic trash can outside the back door, tied the Wal-Mart bag in a knot at the top, and let the chickens fall to the bottom. I decided I'd remove them once I knew where to remove them too.

The rest of the day passed rather blissfully. I took the dogs on our daily walk and sat outside reading in the hammock for the rest of the afternoon. Every now and then, I would look at the blue trash can of death and shudder to think of those six lost chicks who were now laying in a discarded pile at the bottom. Why hadn't he called yet? Oh well, he'll call before tomorrow.

He didn't and as I walked humming out to the barn I knew today would be better. Wrong again. The first brooder I checked had three more dead chicks, the second had another two, and the third had another two. There was also a very tiny chick stumbling its way around in one of the brooders. I knew what that meant. He would be among the count tomorrow. This was becoming way more than "a few" and the tears flowed in streams down my face as I carried these chicks out to the trash can in another Wal-Mart bag.

"You guys deserved so much better than this," I said quietly as I dropped the bag on top of the first one. I tried Pennsylvania again, but still got no response. I sat back and looked at the barn again. Why was I here? I can't do this. I couldn't even keep goldfish alive for crying out loud and now I have "a few" dead chicks and know nothing about what to do with them. I looked up at the sky and started to laugh as I remembered the argument I had with my mom.

"A few is three honey," mom said and tried not to laugh.

"No way mom," I argued, "A few is like seven or eight. I want a few quarters for the arcade tomorrow."

"That is why I gave you three. One is one, a couple is two, and a few is three."

"Well that stinks. That's only three games of skee ball."

My mom walked away from me and laughed under her breath. She used to tell that story to everyone and promised to tell my children someday too.

By the third day, I lumbered out to the barn. The death toll was up to thirteen and I dreaded opening up the brooders. The first held two dead chicks, and they were in unique states of death. The first was completely flat and had been trampled on probably all night. It had no feathers left and it was bent in the oddest of shapes. I didn't even worry about the gloves anymore. I just got it out of there. The other was bloated. Its eyes were purple, closed, and bulging. It looked like one of those stress reliever toys that you squeeze in your hands, but the air got stuck in its head. I would have gagged, but I had no emotions. The next brooder had one dead chick and it was under the heat lamp so it was pretty crispy. I wondered why taxidermy had never thought of using heat. This showed the magic a bit of hot light could do to a dead bird. The last brooder had another three dead chicks. The first was all alone in the corner. I recognized it as the stumbling runt from yesterday. Why the others left it alone I'll never know, but they did. The second was in the water and it looked like none of the other chicks could get water because the dead one took up so much space. After removing those two, I saw the last one. Its one wing was completely exposed bones and as I tried to pick it up the other chicks started pecking me and it fiercely. I started screaming at them, but they proceeded to attack me and the dead chick until I got the lid back on the brooder. I walked out to trash can and after making my third deposit, my cell phone rang. I struggled to get the phone out, but I did before the last ring.

"Hello?"

"Hi Honey, how are you? Sorry, I've been very busy and I couldn't call until now."

"Sure. Did you get any of my messages?"

"No. I just saw you called a bunch of times. What's up?"

That's when I lost it. I sobbed my way through different states of dead chickens, Wal-Mart bags, being a failure, and not knowing how to bury dead chickens when I heard the laughter.

"Nineteen is not bad at all for your first days. That's actually pretty good."

"Pretty good? You said a few, "my anger was starting to rise after being ignored for three days and worrying about the mortality of barnyard fowl, "A few is like three!"

"Yeah, well, I knew you would freak if I said you'd lose more than that, so..."

"So what do I do with them?" I asked quickly.

"You still have the dead ones?"

It was then that I really explained the Wal-Mart bags and the blue trash can of death by the back door.

"Just throw them out in the back forty and the raccoons and such will get them."

"You want me to pitch the dead chickens out in the field?"

"Yeah, why?"

"I can't do that. I can't just start throwing dead chickens around."

"You could build a fire..." the phone cut off and I was left in silence.

A fire I could do. I got some wood and the pizza box from dinner last night and started a nice little blaze. I went to the death can and pulled out all three bags of chicks. I walked over to the fire with Andie by my heels who was extremely interested in what I was doing. I tossed the bags up and...

This would be a good time for a bit of a scientific explanation that I did not know at that point in my life. Fire melts plastic quickly. Fire melts thin Wal-Mart bags even faster than regular plastic.

So, I watched as the plastic bags disintegrated and all of the dead, disfigured baby chickens fell out around the fire. I had to walk around and throw every single dead body into the fire. Afterwards, I stood there and sang quietly...
Day is done,
Gone the sun,
From the lake,
From the hills,
From the sky;
All is well,
Safely rest,
God is nigh.

It's funny. The house and the farm smelled like fried chicken for weeks and to this day that newly made farm girl can't eat fried chicken.

The American Dream
The Beginning
Kimberly Combs

The great depression was in a downward spiral; and everyone thought that it would never get any better, including Isabelle, but she was a person who always looked at life in a positive way; she never let the thought of losing everything get in her way. She still had her father and her sister and niece. People were starving everywhere, but still this did not discourage Isabelle or frighten her even when her father had to leave the farm for work. He traveled among most Americans to find ample employment. Frank, Isabelle's father had to travel across country to lead the build of the hoover dam, this is where his skills came to life. While he was away Isabelle and her sister, Mary, were in charge of the family farm they resided at.

Isabelle was an attractive young lady, her brown hair flowing past her knees, her blue eyes shining like the sky. While she worked on the farm she wore her hair tightly in a bun to keep it out of the way. She wore long dresses as women did in the thirties and very light makeup. She was respectful and kind to everyone she met, but people were starting to talk. They said that she didn't have a family to claim as her own; no husband or children to speak of. Isabelle ignored their stares and rude comments and went on her with her business. She didn't have much interest in the boys that were still left in her town. These men wanted a wife for a homemaker, but Isabelle had better plans; she had a bigger purpose. Her sister already settled down and had a daughter. That life wasn't for Isabelle.

Mary had shoulder length brown hair, and stood a bit taller than Isabelle. She also wore long dresses but had no need to wear her hair in a bun for it was short enough to keep out of the way.

For sisters they got along as best as they knew how, and sometimes they were best friends, but Mary always thought that there was something off with Isabelle. Isabelle had some crazy ideas she would go on about. Women of those days didn't have too many ideas of their own, it wasn't proper. A woman was supposed to help her husband, take care of the children and the house; however Isabelle had her own plans and ideas of how she would live her life.

It was just the three of them at the farm, since Isabelle's mother had passed away while giving birth to her twenty five years before. With the great depression knocking at their door and their father away, they were in charge. They had to do everything in their power to keep the farm afloat. This included selling some of their cows; they only had two left, but two was good for them. Mary's husband, John, also traveled with Frank to lend a hand where needed. They also had to let their servants go. With no money to pay them they couldn't afford the help. Things were changing fast.

The farm was spacious with only the three of them there it felt like a mansion to them. The property had a tool shed, a barn for the cows, chickens and other animals that decided to call it home and a two story farm house, with a new indoor bathroom. There was also four bedrooms which was a lot to them. In the kitchen was an electric stove, which the family was still getting used to and an icebox, a farm sink with a pump that poured water into the sink or a bucket for baths. The family had a telephone installed before Frank went off to Nevada and it was placed next to the kitchen table, this way if he needed to call he could. The bathroom had a huge green cast iron tub that Isabelle or Mary had to carry water to, to fill up since there was only one water pump in the house. The sink was a small pedestal sink that also was green. Isabelle always thought of herself as lucky to have indoor plumbing, because just a few short years before they had an outhouse for a bathroom.

Frank taught Isabelle and Mary how to live off the land, this came in handy when they had to tend to the farm themselves with no help. Their father would also take them hunting and fishing. The words he spoke often was, "The hell with excuses, get results!" They listened very well to him, they never complained and they always did their work with pride. Another thing Frank would say is "Take pride in your work, even if it is shoveling cow manure." Isabelle knew that he never liked the work done half fast.

Mary missed her father and husband, but she occupied her mind by looking after Isabelle, who surely needed it. Isabelle would get the craziest ideas in her head and instead of thinking it though she would act on it.

Isabelle's ideas were to find ways to increase production on certain chores; for instance milking their two cows. Isabelle believed that time was a precious commodity that couldn't be reversed; she wanted to make the most out of life. So while working on the farm she would create ways to make tasks a little simpler, most of the time her experiments worked, but other times it would be a disaster waiting to happen. Even so she tried making a pump for milking their cows, they would sometimes kick the bucket over or even the stool she was sitting on; milking could take hours. The pump was designed to help this process go a little more smoothly, and if it worked correctly she would make more, and possibly sell them to others. Cleverly after she attached the pump to the teat of the first cow, she flipped the switch on. "Oh no!" Isabelle noticed the cows' eyes light up with wild amazement, the bucket went flying, than the cow's hind legs starting kicking outward like a bull would do trying to free himself from the rider. Isabelle ran to the entrance of the barn to get out of harm's way.

"What on God's green earth is going on in here?" Mary shouted while catching her breath, she seemed to appear out of nowhere. Her eyes were filled with fury. She looked at Isabelle and then looked at the cow, it was too freaked to let either one of the girls milk it. Isabelle was speechless; she didn't know how to handle Mary when she was in this kind of mood. But Isabelle thought to herself maybe the cow just didn't like the way the pump squeezed when it was turned on. Isabelle decided to put this experiment on hold for a while; she had to figure a way to make the pump more comfortable so the cow could handle it.

That very night, after the cow incident, Isabelle had a vivid dream of her mother; she looked so beautiful, just like in the pictures her father had shown her. In the dream Isabelle's mother was wearing a long sleek white dress, she appeared to be an angel from heaven but her eyes looked so empty, they showed no emotion. Isabelle heard her mother speak, so plain as if the dream was not a dream and her mother was standing over her bedside speaking directly to her.

"Isabelle come to me, my child, come be with me." At that moment Isabelle's mother reached out her arms and embraced her. Isabelle sat straight up in bed her palms were sweaty and her blanket was damp.

"What are you doing Isabelle?" exclaimed her niece, Roberta. Roberta was only nine but she was very mature, helping the elders on the farm forced her to grow up quickly.

"Just had a dream dear, go back to sleep." But that was easier said than done for Isabelle, her mind still focused on her weird experience from the other side. She rubbed her eyes and blinked a few times, the darkness of the room was coming in a little more clearer now. She threw her covers off, put her bare feet on the wood floor and walked in the dark down the stairs to the kitchen. The clock on the wall read 3:40, she had to be up in an hour to start her daily routine; milking the cows, collecting eggs from the chickens, cleaning all the animal pens and feeding them as well. There was no way she could get back to sleep.

Isabelle grabbed the tin tea kettle; put it under the faucet and pumped water into it until it was full, and then placed it on the stove, while she waited for the kettle to whistle, she got down a tea cup and a tea bag. A few minutes later the steam was rising out of the kettle with a warning signal that the water was ready. She finished her tea in no time then decided to start her chores early, she was a person who didn't like to waste any time.

The sun beat hot on her skin that day, giving her a reason to escape to the water hole to cool off. The water was just right, she pulled up her dress, kicked off her boots and stepped in. Never caring that her clothes would get a little wet. She dipped her hands under the water and pulled some out in a cup like fashion, she splashed her face and as she did this, she looked down into the reflection of the water; she almost fainted. Her mother was staring back at her with a crooked smile and a slight wink.

Isabelle returned to her chores but couldn't get her mother off her mind, or the dream for that matter. She didn't dare tell her family about the dream or what she witnessed in the water hole, she didn't want them to think she was insane, more than they already did. Isabelle knew what would become of her if they found out. She heard of people that saw certain things that no one else saw and they wouldn't be believed, so the people would send them away.

Isabelle couldn't get her mind free from her own imagination. The dream repeated itself for a week or more. Isabelle had bags under her eyes and dark circles too. She would find herself falling asleep milking the cows or at the dinner table, her family noticed but they didn't mention it to her.

"I can't stand it any longer," Isabelle said to herself. "I need to resolve this before I lose my mind, my chores are not getting the attention they deserve and I haven't had a good night sleep in weeks. I have to do something about this."

Isabelle stomped off to the tool shed, she closed the wooden door behind her and stroke a match to light the lantern that was sitting on the work bench. She looked around and decided to use exactly that, the oversized work bench would suit her for her tasks to come. She didn't have much wiggle room in the shed but she would make it work, the work bench took up most of the space; she would have to stand while she worked. Since Isabelle couldn't put her daily chores on hold she would have to wake up before the sun and go to bed when the moon was at its highest. There was a long road ahead for Isabelle and she was determined to find out how to make the dream stop.

She cleared off the bench and started collecting the materials she needed for this long process. She grabbed a huge pot from the kitchen, the kind that a family would use to cook for a big gathering, a few wooden spoons, a funnel from a shelve in the shed, and her notebook from her room. She filled the pot up to the brim with water and carried it carefully back to the tool shed without spilling a drop. Isabelle was not new to experiments, she liked to see what things she could create if she mixed certain ingredients together. Isabelle always dreamed of going to school to become more than just a nurse or a secretary, but she knew that would never happen. She wanted to become a scientist, but women were not allowed. She taught herself many things behind everyone's back, her mind always wondered with new ideas.

A few years ago Isabelle accidently made a healing product; it was to close up freshly cut skin and help the bleeding to stop. What she was trying to do instead, was tape a picture back together, but the middle had a piece of an adhesive missing, this did not work, the picture wouldn't stay together. She then realized that she had cut her finger on the paper, it only bled a little but she wanted to close it up. She picked up the piece of tape and wrapped it around her finger where the cut was visible. This not only made the bleeding stop, but it also took some of the pain away because of the pressure it was providing. Isabelle always worked hard for what she wanted and she desperately wanted to have a lot of knowledge, she read a lot of books and studied hard.

For months Isabelle worked on her new project. She would wake up and creep down the stairs careful not to make a sound.

Isabelle milked the cows with the recreated pump; she was able adjust it just right to fit the cows properly. It only took a couple of tries to get it right. This pump didn't scare the cows anymore. Most days she could finish her tasks in half the time it used to take; when they were complete she escaped to the tool shed. She would look around to make sure no one was watching her walk in that direction. It was her secret and hers alone, that was until Roberta walked into the shed, "supper's on the tab..." Roberta cut her sentence short; she was filled with shock and wonder at the sight. There were glass bottles and funnels spread out on the work bench and a small fire was burning near the large pot. The smell was horrid, it was that of a dead animal, but Roberta hoped it was something different.

Roberta's mouth hung open; wide enough to catch big bugs, and her eyes were just as wide. Isabelle looked straight at Roberta and instantly spoke, "You can't tell your ma you hear? And if papa phones in you can't mention it to him either. Promise me, this is our little secret. Promise me Roberta." Isabelle looked straight into Roberta's eyes and held her by the shoulders, not too tight to where it would hurt her but enough to frighten the child. She had to bend a little to be face to face with her. Roberta swore that she wouldn't tell, and for a reward Isabelle made her the assistant on this secret project.

Roberta always received good grades in school; science was her favorite subject, so it wasn't any surprise when she knew what Isabelle was talking about when they worked together. Roberta always wore very beautiful dresses that hung to her feet and since the family was poor from the loss of their money, Roberta mostly got hand me downs from her mother or her aunt and they had to adjust the length so it wouldn't drag on the floor. Unlike her aunt or her mother, Roberta had shoulder length sun bleached hair, which most likely came from her grandmother; no one else in the family had her type of hair.

Six months went by since Roberta first walked into the shed uninvited and almost a year since Isabelle first started the project. It was time for Isabelle to test her solution on rats. They were at abundance on the farm; they would chew through cardboard boxes and leave their droppings everywhere. Isabelle thought, at least they can be useful now. After quite some time she came up with the name Nostalgia for her solution, which was more like a drug than anything else. Nostalgia was supposed to get injected into the vein of a person's arm with a three inch needle, but trying to find a vein on a small rat with that long of a needle was tricky. Isabelle managed to find a vein after attempting serval times, she finally succeed. The only names she gave the rats were R1, R2, R3 and so on, she didn't want to form an attachment to them.

The results from the tests were not clear until another six months had passed; Isabelle wasn't even sure what she was looking for until it happened.

They were on the 15th rat, Isabelle was hoping for results on this one, but when she injected him with the Nostalgia solution she became disappointed once again because nothing happened. She had left the shed with her head hung low. She felt like such a failure that she excused herself to the washroom so that she could be by herself and think.

After a little while by herself, she returned, all calm and collected. She noticed that R15 was not in his cage. She looked straight at Roberta who didn't notice because her face was buried in a book. Roberta didn't even notice that the rat was missing and this outraged Isabelle, "Where's R15 Roberta? What did you do with him?!" Isabelle tried hard to keep her anger under control.

"Huh?" Replied Roberta, very confused. She casted a glance and took in the fact that the cage was still latched, Isabelle noticed as well, and they were both filled with wonder and amazement. Isabelle calmed down almost instantly, she decided to work on another rat and wait to see what happens with R15. Sometime had passed and while they were concentrating on R16 they heard a squeak coming from R15's cage, instantly they looked over and the rat was exactly where they had left it before. It was like an invisible hand sat him back in the cage.

There was only one difference, R15 looked as though he was more aware of his surroundings as if he had been there in the past, he didn't look like he aged one bit either. Isabelle set up the maze they used on the rats before and after the injection, she picked up R15 from his cage, she placed him at the beginning and then grabbed her stop watch that her grandfather gave her. She lifted the cardboard stopper as she hit the start button on the watch. The rat took off and didn't stop until he was at the end, it didn't even take him ten seconds, dramatically less than before the injection where he ran the maze in three minutes. At that moment Isabelle acted like a child on Christmas morning reaching out for Roberta and jumping with joy.

Roberta was jumping with her aunt but she was a little confused again, she didn't understand why Isabelle was so happy. The rat only learned how to do the maze better, but just then a light bulb came on in her head, she understood. R15 went into the past and learned how to do the maze at a faster pace. When he returned to his original time he brought that knowledge back with him. Isabelle also learned something; the Nostalgia solution/drug would wear off after a while.

The dream of her mother was still clear in Isabelle's mind, the one true item that motivated her in all she did. It was time to tell her niece what started this crazy journey. She sat her down on the dirt floor to explain it all. When the story was finished they both stood up abruptly. IT WAS TIME!

Isabelle had completed the testing; now it was on to the final phase. She had to use the drug on herself and hope beyond hope that she will be with her mother once again. Before she took the injection to her vein, she looked straight into Roberta's blue eyes; the words got caught in her throat, but she was finally able to speak. "Roberta, my sweet, sweet niece, this is very important and so far you have kept your secret like you have promised, but if anything shall go wrong you have to fetch your mother and promise me that this family will stand strong, if the worst happens. And if my soul leaves my body but my flesh is still here make sure the family takes care of me." Roberta put her hand to her mouth and gasped, Isabelle didn't want to frighten Roberta but she needed to inform her of the backup plan that was set in place in case something tragic happened.

Roberta returned the look Isabelle was giving her, she wanted to make sure that she took her seriously when she said, "I promise, I'll do what you asked."

Isabelle took the syringe into her right hand, shaking slightly, but trying to control it. She took the needle, stuck it in the blueish substance that was sitting in a small tube, then she pulled back on the syringe until it was filled. She breathed in slowly and then let it out with a loud sigh. Relieved and nervous that it was coming to this point. It was finally here!

She swallowed hard one more time, took in a deep breath, she thought her heart would explode right out of her chest. She lifted her long sleeve on her left arm to find the vein she had already prepared by marking with a pen. This was it. She carefully lined up the needle and stabbed her vein with a bit of force to make sure it got in deep. She then pushed the syringe slowly, careful not to get air bubbles in her vein. Isabelle was thankful that she read a lot to understand how to use a needle. Even reading was not common for women but Isabelle wanted to educate herself.

Not even five minutes later, Isabelle felt faint, the world was spinning. Then without any warning she hit the dirt floor with so much force, some of the rat cages fell to the floor and busted open.

Roberta ran to the house to retrieve her mother. "Mother! Mother! Come quick Isabelle has fallen ill!" Roberta shouted while running to the house.

Mother and Daughter ran to the shed. Mary saw Isabelle laying on the floor, her face was as pale as a ghost, her eyes were closed but Mary saw that her chest was moving up and down in a breathing motion; she ran back to the house to call the doctor, leaving Roberta to look after Isabelle. The doctor was there in no time at all. His diagnosis was that Isabelle had fallen into a deep sleep, the doctor didn't have the slightest idea of when she would wake or how it happened, Roberta already covered her left arm. The doctor carried her up the stairs and laid her in bed.

Roberta's face could show the struggle she was holding back, she swallowed hard and spoke in a low voice, "Mother, Isabelle was working on a way to get to the past to meet her, your mother, she told me to promise that we would take care of her if something bad happened. It was a drug she took." At that moment Roberta lifted Isabelle's sleeve where the needle had stuck her.

From that day on they would visit her and read to her. The doctor brought over supplies that could help her get nutrition. Mary also flipped her from side to side because they didn't want her to get bed sores. This was a task that Roberta could not do for her aunt until she was a bit older.

THE DISCOVERY

Days turned into weeks, weeks turned into months, and months turned into years. The family still had hoped that one day she would open her eyes and smile up at them. But that time didn't come. Until one afternoon...

Isabelle opened her eyes slowly; she must have moved the sheets because that was the only sound that was present. This made the girl sitting next to her turn and look in her direction. The words were trapped in Isabelle's mind they would not escape her lips. She tried again after a thick swallow, but again nothing came out. She saw a cup of water placed on the night stand, she moved her eyes in that direction and the girl noticed, she grabbed it and gave Isabelle a sip from the straw.

"Roberta, wha... wha... what happened?" The girl ran out of the room to fetch her mother. A few minutes later they both appeared but only standing in the doorway, almost like they were afraid to come in.

Isabelle spoke once more, "Mary is that you? Come closer." Her voice was harsh.

The lady in the doorway was hesitant but she did what Isabelle asked. Now it was her turn to speak. "My name is Alexa, I am Roberta's great grandchild, and this is Grace, she is my daughter. This may come as a shock to you, but you have been asleep for 83 years, we almost lost hope that you would never come back to the family. There is so much to be said."

Ha a shock, Isabelle thought. This is a nightmare!! Alexa could tell that Isabelle was a little shocked from the news that was just spoken, so she took it a step further in hopes of comforting her.

Alexa continued to speak, "We have your journals. Roberta even wrote in the last one, you told her to keep you out of the rest homes and we honored that wish, we also know that you tried to go into the past to meet your deceased mother, now the only question we have for you is; did you get there while you were sleeping?" She was referring to the past.

Isabelle was speechless; they only wanted to know if she got to meet her mother. When she looked around she could tell that she was in her own bedroom, there were only a few changes she noticed right away. There was a big black flat thing hanging on the wall in front of the bed. She didn't have a clue to what that might be, also the clothes that Alexa and Grace were wearing were disgraceful; tight and showed too much skin.

Finally words formed on her tongue and she spoke. "I don't think I got there, and if I did I don't remember it." She said with a very sad look on her face. That was all she wanted was to meet the person who brought her into this world, and now she is somewhere eighty-three years in the future. A thought popped into her brain, was she old, she didn't sound old. "May I see a mirror?" Isabelle demanded, Alexa told Grace to get one from the bathroom.

When she returned she handed the mirror to Isabelle. It took her a minute to get the courage to hold the mirror up to her face. She took a breath and held it while putting the mirror in front of her. Nothing had changed, except for maybe a whiter complexion, and a tad bit skinnier. At that moment Isabelle's stomach roared with sounds of hunger. Alexa went into the kitchen to make Isabelle a sandwich. While Isabelle ate Alexa took the IV out of Isabelle's arm, this little piece of equipment kept her alive all these years.

After she ate, she handed the mirror back to Alexa and threw off the covers, she thought she would have a hard time standing after eighty-three years of not walking, so she took it very slow. She put one foot down and surprisingly she had feeling in it, then came the other foot. She took a step forward and walked just fine. The drug seem to give her abnormal abilities. She didn't age or loose strength, but it didn't work like it was supposed to. She wanted to go to the past not the future. She was outraged and frightened at this thought

"I want to see Mary, my sister!" Isabelle couldn't believe that she was talking so rude, "please." she added.

"Isabelle, it is eighty-three years later, your sister and niece have passed away. I know this is heart breaking for you." Isabelle almost fell to the floor, she felt light headed and couldn't catch her breath but Alexa caught her and sat her back on the four post bed.

Her brain kept running with crazy thoughts, I didn't say goodbye, I didn't do everything I was supposed to with them. My life is over!! The horrible thoughts of quilt just kept coming, they wouldn't stop. Alexa saw the confusion that was appearing on Isabelle's face. Alexa sat next to Isabelle and put her arm around her shoulder, this made Isabelle feel like a child, she didn't know Alexa so she was tense, she felt as though she was a stranger who awoke in a strange house somewhere in the future, but in reality she was in her house with her own family.

Alexa didn't let Isabelle leave the room for some time; Isabelle felt like she was in a prison, a comfortable prison, but a prison none the less. Alexa tried to explain that the world had changed since 1931, but Isabelle didn't want to hear it. She just wanted the sun on her face and feel the wind blow through her hair.

Two weeks had passed; Isabelle had learned a little bit from Alexa. She learned how many presidents were in office since 1931, and now there was a black president in office. She also learned that the item hanging on the wall was a television, they were in almost every home. She already seen how the women of this decade dressed, she was uncomfortable about that, she was more proper than that. She also learned about cell phones and how they worked. All this new technology seemed so confusing. But there was something interesting she learn among all the confusing items. The pump that she used to milk her two cows was actually an item sold to farmers everywhere. This was how Alexa could afford the farm house and stay at home to take care of her only daughter.

Isabelle wanted to be along with her thoughts, "You mentioned that you kept my journals, may I see them please? I would like to write some notes on what you are telling me." Isabelle stated while Alexa was giving her more information about the future. She also wanted to read her old notes from her era. She wanted desperately to get back to her time, but didn't know where to start since these young ladies wouldn't let her leave this bedroom. But she wouldn't speak a word about that, not yet anyway. Alexa went to retrieve her journals and left Isabelle to read.

The day finally came when Alexa opened the door and stated, "Let's go for a walk." She thought that Isabelle was ready to face the future.

Isabelle was shocked at this statement but glad she was finally able to leave the bedroom, she had to prepare herself first. She needed to take a bath, and brush her hair. Before Alexa left the room Isabelle stopped her. "Can you please bring me water from the kitchen so I can take a bath first, I feel so filthy."

Alexa looked at her with a puzzled look, she didn't know what Isabelle meant, bring her water? Alexa than thought that everything is new to Isabelle. She decided that she would have to teach her just like she would have to teach a toddler. "Follow me, I am going to show you something different then you are used to."

With a little hesitation Isabelle followed Alexa into the bathroom, it looked so different. The green tub was replaced with a white shiny one and there were many more items surrounding it.

"I believe that when you had to take baths, you had to get water from the kitchen to fill up the tub, is that correct Isabelle?" Alexa asked.

Isabelle just nodded in response. Alexa then explained that in 2014 water came when a person turned a knob or two and adjusted the tempature by just messing with those knobs. "Then you just turn the middle knob to have water come out of the shower head, that's this object, right here." Alexa pointed to the sprayer hanging on the shower wall.

All this new information was really confusing Isabelle, but she didn't let on. It seemed easy enough, until Alexa left and she messed with the knobs herself. First it was too cold than slightly too hot, after a while it was good enough to take a "shower". Than it was time to use the soap.

There were so many sitting on the edge of the tub, which one was she supposed to use? She picked up one at a time and read them. The shampoo was used for washing her hair, but there were a few different ones with different scents. Isabelle choose the lavender scent; washed her hair quickly and then she thought she was done when she glimpsed at another bottle sitting next to the shampoo. This one read conditioner, she read this label, it said it was a rinse aid. She put this in her hair and stepped out of the shower. Her hair felt greasy, but she figured this is what the 2014 people live like. This process seemed a little easier to Isabelle, than taking all that water and carrying it to the tub, but a little more confusing.

When she dried off Isabelle located a brush that was placed next to the sink, she brushed her long hair quickly not caring if she missed a knot here or there. Eighty-three years had passed; she wanted to make up for lost time. In doing so she didn't want to spend it brushing her hair. Isabelle dressed quickly and walked out into the hall where Alexa and Grace were waiting.

The clothes she was wearing seemed so tight and different. The pants stuck to her legs while she was walking, she didn't like the feeling of this and kept stopping to pull at them, and her shirt was so low cut, her bra was almost showing, this made her feel uncomfortable. The clothes were so different from her time; it almost felt unreal, like she was on an alien planet.

"We're taking a small walk around the property today and maybe a little longer one tomorrow if all goes well." Alexa said to Isabelle and Grace before opening the back door.

Before she stepped out the door, Isabelle looked around the newly remodeled house. Everything looked so different, but they said this was her old farm house. The furniture looked something like a person would have in a space ship. The couches had no arms or backs and the chairs had electric buttons to move the leg rest up and down. The icebox looked like something that belonged on a shuttle too. It had a device that held freshly made ice that you could put in your cup any time you wanted ice water or any beverage cold, and it was huge, why would anyone need so much food? A person would have to keep so much ice in it to keep the items cold all day. Then Isabelle looked at the walls, they were painted bold colors, where Isabelle was used to yellow everywhere. Some were painted bright pink and others a pastel blue or purple.

At this point Grace grabbed her arm and said, "Auntie, let's go for a walk, you need some fresh air, come on."

Auntie? What kind of word is that? Isabelle didn't understand, it was so foreign to her. But for right now she just lifted up her shoulders to shrug it off. There was already too much to digest.

She took one step onto the back porch, not knowing what to expect. The heat was intense and the light almost blinded her. As soon as her eyes adjusted she looked around, the shed was still there, where she worked on Nostalgia. The wood was peeling badly and the roof looked to have never been repaired, and it almost looked as though it was leaning to one side.

The barn was also still standing, but Isabelle couldn't hear soft mooing sounds or smell manure. She ran in that direction with all her might, running faster and faster, but when she reached the barn she paused. Alexa thought she was just trying to catch her breath, but in truth Isabelle was afraid of what she was going to see as soon as she walked in.

Isabelle's feeling was right, the cows were gone and all that was left was a pile of junk stacked high. Old tools and equipment filled the barn where the cows had been, supplying the family with fresh milk.

The next place Isabelle escaped to was the shed. She didn't dare step inside, not knowing if it would cave in on her. She peeked inside, it was bare, the dirt floor was still visible, and her work bench where she once worked her fingers to the bone was also bare. All her rats and jugs were gone, disappeared!

Isabelle fell to her knees not knowing where her strength was, that had also disappeared. Alexa ran to her but Isabelle pushed her away, she just wanted to be left alone, to dwell into the past. This was the first day being out in the world and so far it wasn't looking good. The farm had changed drastically, all her belongings gone.

"Isabelle your items are locked in the basement." Alexa whispered when she found it appropriate. At that moment Isabelle found her strength and stood once more, hope was reappearing, she may be able to get to her time and be with the ones she loved.

Alexa and Grace helped her back to her room to rest; they said they can try again the following day. Little did they know that it would storm the next day. Isabelle tossed and turned all that night with little hope of sleep, thoughts kept coming and leaving a sting inside Isabelle's heart. The rain didn't discourage Isabelle, she borrowed a rain coat from Alexa, and went forth on a little adventurer, comparing the past with the future.

Isabelle did not have a panic attack this time, she had no hopes of seeing the way things used to be, she finally understood that it was so far in the future that nothing would ever be the same again.

A few weeks went by since her first initial step into the unknown. She finally got used to her knew wardrobe and almost got used to her new but old surroundings.

She may have been getting used to this new place, but she still didn't like it. There was not a man living in the house and Alexa explained that her and her husband got a divorce a few years ago, this was not common to Isabelle, in her day a man and a woman stayed together through thick and thin. But Isabelle saw that in this era a marriage was not that important to couples, once they got tired of each other they were gone. Back in her time divorce wasn't an option.

After supper every night Alexa and Grace would plop down in front of the television set to watch shows or sometimes "reruns", Isabelle didn't understand how the television worked, she figured it was the same way a radio worked. She didn't join them, she shrugged her shoulders at that thought, what's the point of watching other people's lives, I have my own life to get back to.

Isabelle barely talked to Alexa, but with Grace it was different. Grace wanted to know all about the past and what it was like. Most days Isabelle didn't mind the company but other days she worked on her journals to get the formula correct, she needed quietness to concentrate.

Knock knock, Isabelle heard a knock at her bedroom door; she sat down her book and slowly went to see who was knocking. "Hey Isabelle, Grace and I were thinking that maybe you would like to join us tonight? See it's the first of the month and this is our date night."

Date night? Isabelle thought to herself, isn't that with a man and a woman? But Isabelle didn't care she wanted out of the house, "Yes that would be lovely."

Before they left the house Alexa said, "Isabelle, if anyone asks you are my cousin from Florida, you are here to visit. No one knows that you were in our house all this time, we were careful." Isabelle just nodded her head not knowing what to say to this.

Too many secrets she thought, she never told the girls that she was planning to go back to her time; she didn't want them to worry or stop her.

Isabelle was riding up front with Alexa in her red G6, the radio was playing a song, Isabelle couldn't make out the lyrics because the singer was going way to fast. She also noted that he was using profanity with almost every sentence. "What kind of music is this Alexa? It's awful."

Alexa reached forward and changed the station to something more Isabelle's liking, country. When they finally arrived at the restaurant, their bellies were growling so loudly that everyone in the car could hear. This made them smile.

Alexa parked the car and they walked in together. The hostess was standing in front of them in less than a second. "How many?"

"Three please." Alexa said. They followed her and was seated by the window. They were handed menus and asked what they would like to drink.

Isabelle didn't bother looking at the menu for drinks, she just ordered a water, Alexa a coffee and Grace ordered a coke. This shocked Isabelle because respectable girls didn't have soda at dinner, they would get that at special occasions, they should get milk or juice. She bit her tongue; she didn't dare tell someone else how to raise their child, especially since she didn't know how people did things in this day and age.

Isabelle almost spit out her water when she looked at the menu, THE PRICES, everything was for a rich person. She looked at the steak prices, she was outraged, twenty dollars for one steak and a baked potato. Why would Alexa bring her to such an expensive place. She kept her cool and sat down the menu. She whispered over to Alexa who was still looking over the menu, "I can't find anything that doesn't cost an arm and a leg." Isabelle took another sip of water hoping that it didn't cost as much. She was surprised she didn't see anything under five dollars. When she had a steak dinner in the 30's it was a dollar and twenty five cents, not twenty dollars. That seemed outrageous to her.

Alexa tried to tell her that, prices are a lot different from her time, but Isabelle still was careful of what she ordered. A salad was the only thing on the menu that wouldn't break the bank, she thought anyway.

When they finished eating, Alexa grabbed the bill and walked up to pay. It wasn't cash she used though, it was a plastic card. Another weird difference. And then in the car on the way home she noticed more; the gas prices were sky high, and even Alexa agreed with her on that one. That day they were almost three dollars a gallon, Alexa said that some days it gets close to four dollars a gallon. Again Isabelle compared prices, in her time it was ten cents per gallon.

For the rest of the evening Isabelle kept to herself. She had a lot of thinking to do. A whole night went by without so much as Isabelle setting her head on the pillow. She was desperate; she wanted to get back to her "family" the ones she grew up with. She missed her sister and her father and most importantly her little niece. It came to her, she needed to ask for help whether she liked it or not.

She swallowed her pride, opened her bedroom door and walked down the stairs to the kitchen where she could hear Alexa cooking breakfast. She took a seat at the breakfast bar. Alexa noticed and stopped abruptly. "Is everything okay Isabelle?"

"No it's not Alexa, I need to ask for something and when I do, you need to be open minded." She took a breath and waited for Alexa's response, all she got was a nod but that was good enough. "I want to go home, and before you interrupt, this is my home but not my time, I want to go back to my time, with my sister and my niece. I want to see my father return home. I can't do it alone. I have been looking at my journals and I believe I know what went wrong, and with today's technology I can fix it. I can go back." She sat up straight getting ready for her to deny her this opportunity. But that's not what happened.

"Ok Isabelle, let's do it!" Alexa didn't mean to use so much excitement in her voice, and Isabelle almost thought that she wanted her gone just as much as she wanted to be gone. The task of taking care of her must have been hard on her. Isabelle couldn't help but wonder if the stress of caring for her may have had something to do with her divorce.

Little Grace was at school; Alexa and Isabelle got started right away. All of Isabelle's old supplies were stored in the basement, they both went to fetch them, it took a few trips but finally they collected all what they needed. They placed the materials in the study; this would become Isabelle's new laboratory.

Isabelle than grabbed her journals and placed them nearby. A little while later, after running to the store for some more supplies, Isabelle got started mixing what she needed. Isabelle still had all the memories of before she fell into her coma. She remember that she had so much intelligence it made her family believe that she was strange, like an ugly duckling. Alexa hooked up a boom box with quiet music, some old tunes that Isabelle would be used to. She had to break the tension that was filling the room.

Since Isabelle did this once before it didn't take too long before she had the solution mixed in a beaker. It was time to test it on the rats. This was a struggle because the stray cats had taken care of most of them. They did however find a few in the basement.

All this was done before Grace got home. When she walked through the door Alexa walked out of the study and locked it behind her, they didn't want her involved with this.

The only break Isabelle took was when dinner was prepared. After dinner Grace was left to her homework and Isabelle went back to her project. It didn't take as long as it once did for the solution to get to the testing stage and they already had a rat in a cage to test on. Again Isabelle named the rats R1 and so on. R1 was big, brown and full of energy. It took several tries to find a vein, like before.

Isabelle found one and jammed the needle into the creature. She took out the stop watch Alexa let her borrow, set it, and just waited. Not even five minutes later the rat disappeared, and then two minutes it returned, she didn't even bother doing the maze on this rat.

She had to try this on a bigger creature; this was the problem she had before. She went from rats to herself and didn't test it on a bigger animal. Alexa said they had stray cats hanging around. Isabelle grabbed a can of tuna; stepped outside, placed the can on the back step and waited. A couple hours later a small orange cat approached the can with caution. Isabelle snuck behind it and scooped it up with ease, at first, but then it started fighting her.

She placed it in the cage next to the rat; both of them didn't like that one bit. Isabelle hurried and grabbed another needle with the solution already in place. She found a vein in the alley cat with no problem. Again she jammed this animal with the needle, with the hope that she would be with her family soon. She then set the stop watch and timed it. By this time the moon was high and everyone was asleep, she didn't care, she didn't want them to see what she was doing to these animals.

About four minutes later the cat disappeared just like the rat. But unlike the rat the cat took even longer to return. Isabelle was losing hope that it would return. Three hours had passed; Isabelle was fast asleep, her head laying on the desk, papers sticking to her face. The sound that woke her was a soft "meow". The cat finally returned, looking scared.

Isabelle wanted to try this new Nostalgia drug, but with a lot of nerves running high she had decided to wait until Grace went to school and had Alexa's undivided attention. This was serious. Isabelle didn't want to end up farther into the future, but she also knew that this era was not for her. People getting divorced, this thing called television that takes everyone's attention, kids disrespecting their elders. She was wondering what happened to the world.

In the time that she spent in the bedroom before exploring the unknown, she learned of her father's death, that he died of TB from the workers at the dam. Even if she was around she couldn't do anything to stop it, but she just wished she could have had more time with him.

Isabelle also learned that Alexa didn't get a divorce just because she had to take care of her; her husband was lazy and didn't want to support the family. She seen how Grace talked to her mom. She was very disrespectful. If her mom asked her to do something Grace would reply with "no mom, I am busy" and so Alexa would do it herself instead of teaching her daughter a lesson. Back in the thirties a child would get punished for talking to their parents like that. All Isabelle wanted was to be back with her family, around the things that made sense. And stay there. No more messing with experiments she doesn't know much about.

Morning finally came, Grace was off to school, it was time. Alexa was ready to help Isabelle go back to her real family. Isabelle found the same vein that she had used in the beginning of this whole process. "Alexa I am going on this journey in hopes that I can be with the people that know me, I need to be back in my time, but if anything happens to me. I do not want you to be burdened by my presence. Please take me to a nice rest home and make sure I am taken care of from time to time. Hopefully this will work and I will meet you when I am an old lady and you are a tiny little tot." Isabelle swallowed down some tears. She was scared but excited. She was hoping beyond hope that this was going to work. "Now give me a hug and let's get this over with."

They hugged hard; Isabelle reached for the needle already filled with the solution. She lifted her sleeve, this was it. The poke was over quick. And a few minutes later Isabelle felt faint, just like before. Oh no, here we go again. Isabelle thought that she was doing exactly what happened before.

Sure enough, Isabelle fainted. She hit the ground hard but didn't feel it; she was already out before she landed. Out cold.

THE RETURN HOME

Isabelle opened her eyes, her nerves were high. She looked around slowly not knowing what she would see. She had already been to the future she didn't want to see more from the future, but that is not what she saw. She saw her own furniture; her own clothes were on her body. There was no weird televisions hanging on the wall, and no weird people staring at her. It was quiet, too quiet. She was able to sit up, but she did this slowly.

She was not sure what to expect; was she back in her time? Or was she in another place in time?

She stepped out of bed very carefully, she walked to the window and looked out at the farm. It was her farm she was looking at, just the way she left it. The tool shed to look in tacked and she could smell the sweet aroma of manure coming from outside. She was home, in her time!

She ran down the stairs, almost tripping over her feet. She found Mary milking the cows; the sight was overwhelming. Isabelle reached out her arms and gave her a big squeeze. "What was that for Isabelle?"

"I missed you, I missed you so much." Isabelle said holding back tears.

"What are you talking about? You just woke up sleepy head. I just seen you last night before you went to bed." Mary's face showed how confused she was. Mary didn't know what Isabelle was going on about.

"I traveled to the future, you and dad and Roberta had already passed away, I couldn't say goodbye. I was there for a few months. I made it back to be with you though. I am never going to let you go again." Isabelle hugged Mary even tighter, almost like a child not wanting to let her mother go.

"Roberta said you were making weird noises while you were sleeping, this is why we let you sleep a little longer, maybe you need just a bit more." Mary said with a smile appearing across her lips.

Maybe it was all just a dream, Isabelle thought. Nothing seemed to be out of sorts, everyone seemed the same as the day she had the dream of her mother. That's it! It was all a dream. Isabelle went to the shed to look around. The tools were on the bench as though she never moved them to work on her project. There was no big pot sitting in there. And when she saw Roberta, she couldn't help herself, she hugged her as well.

"It must have been one crazy dream Aunt Isabelle."

"Oh it was Roberta."

Her family would never know what she had discovered, she would never tell them. The future was like an alien country. She was glad she would be old before she reached that era again. The era of disrespect and laziness. She sat back that evening and enjoyed her families company, without a care in the world. No more experiments unless it was to help someone in need. No more wondering what the past or future held. For now on she was going to focus solely on the present.

Yesterday is history, tomorrow is a mystery.

And today? Today is a gift,

That's why we call it the present.

By Alice Morse Earle

Contributing Authors

Carol Hanson

Carol Hanson

Where are you from?
Rochester Hills, Michigan

When and why did you begin writing?
I have always been an avid reader, and loved expressive language. Sometimes something just comes to me, and I enjoy the flight it takes me on.

What would you say is your most interesting writing quirk?
I can be anywhere, and I will jot down a phrase or words that I think will light up a page.

What do you like to do when you're not writing?
Everything else! I enjoy reading, walking, gardening, photography, and I love the challenge of a good crossword puzzle.

As a child, what did you want to do when you grew up?
Well, one day it would be a nurse, then a stewardess, or maybe a police officer. I would watch a movie, and then be onto another direction altogether.

Christopher Chagnon

Christopher Chagnon

Where are you from?
I was born in the oddly named town of Bad Axe Michigan, 1951.

When and why did you begin writing?
I began writing poetry and anthologies in high school. I guess I was just thinking too much.

What would you say is your most interesting writing quirk?
I'll play my guitar occasionally while I'm shaping a scene or an interesting character I'm creating.

What do you like to do when you're not writing?
I'm drawn to my fishing boat when there is liquid water here in northern Michigan. In the fall, I'll take my two dogs for a hunt without my gun loaded; I love to watch them work a grouse or pheasant out their hiding places. There is always a guitar nearby while I read.

As a child, what did you want to do when you grew up?
I didn't think I'd ever grow up. But when I got to high school, and told my ninth grade English teacher I wanted to be a writer, she suggested I was better suited to becoming a barber. Her remark made me more determined to follow my dream.

Claudia Ivey

Claudia Ivey

Where are you from?
Ferndale, Michigan

When and why did you begin writing?
Always wanted to be. I am a dyslexic that wants to write-had several stories I wanted to write.

What would you say is your most interesting writing quirk?

What do you like to do when you're not writing?
Travel and art

As a child, what did you want to do when you grew up?
Art teacher-storybook illustrator

Dennis Klotz

Dennis Klotz

Where are you from?
Dearborn Heights, Michigan

When and why did you begin writing?
I was always a good story teller, even as a child, but it wasn't until high school that I started writing after taking a creative writing class. My English teacher believed in my writing and nominated me for Most Creative Writer. I never forgot that, and later when I picked up a short story anthology, I realized I wanted to write short stories and that I had a solid foundation to do so. Short stories, when written well, can be just as powerful as novels, and they are also a very demanding form to write in, and that's why I write them. I want to be able to move people through a powerful medium.

What would you say is your most interesting writing quirk?
I always have the ending in mind, and I usually write that first.

What do you like to do when you're not writing?
I read, play guitar, study the world and the people in it, and focus on better myself in all areas of my life.

As a child, what did you want to do when you grew up?
I wanted to be a pirate, then a sailor, then a firefighter, then a musician.

Elizabeth Farney Maxon

Elizabeth Farney Maxon

Where are you from?
I am originally from Dayton, Ohio.

When and why did you begin writing?
I began writing when I was in grade school. I was never very good in art, so I was the kid who asked to write a paper, poem, or story instead of using scissors and glue.

What would you say is your most interesting writing quirk?
I like to revise. I like rereading work and trying to make sure that each word is exactly what I want.

What do you like to do when you're not writing?
When I am not writing, I park hop with my children Isaac (3) and Darcy (10). I also teach ZUMBA choreograph/direct musicals, teach dance, read, and teach high school English.

As a child, what did you want to do when you grew up?
When I was child, among other professions, I wanted to be the first woman Cinicnnati Reds player. I also wanted to be a Rockette and a lawyer.

Kimberly Combs

Kimberly Combs

Where are you from?
I am from Holly, Michigan, born and raised.

When and why did you begin writing?
I began writing as a small child; I enjoyed the thought of being in someone else's shoes, even if it was just for a little while. Creative writing was my favorite subject.

What would you say is your most interesting writing quirk?
I would have to say my most interesting writing quirk is; having my characters talk. I almost feel like I am in the conversation with them.

What do you like to do when you're not writing?
Family is very important to me, so when I am not writing my thoughts on paper I spend time with my kids or my husband. Whom I must say give me a ton of ideas for new stories

As a child, what did you want to do when you grew up?
When I was a child I wanted to be a writer, but as I got older I lost hope of that dream, I didn't think it would be possible. And now that I look back, I wish that I could take it all back and start from the beginning, because besides my family, writing is what I enjoy most of all.

Melissa Grunow

Melissa Grunow

***Where* are you from?**
Ferndale, Michigan

When and why did you begin writing?
I've been writing since I was a teen because I always felt I had a story to tell. A got away from writing for the better part of my twenties, but started up again three years ago because I had memories and moments and stories to *discover*. There is a difference between telling a story and discovering one, and it was when I started approaching writing as a truth-seeking process, I trusted myself more to capture the real substance of a piece.

What would you say is your most interesting writing quirk?
I sketch, outline, and sometimes draft pieces on Post-it notes. I'm always on the go, so when I have an idea, I quickly jot it down, usually on a Post-it. Then when I have a moment in front of the computer, I use the Post-its to start to piece together something new. That way, I'm not wasting time in the writer's chair thinking about writing instead of actually writing.

What do you like to do when you're not writing?
I'm doing some variation of the following: Reading other peoples' writing, home improvement projects, planning my October wedding, spending time with my fiancé and my husky, enjoying summertime in Michigan on outdoor patios, traveling, and participating in live storytelling events.

As a child, what did you want to do when you grew up?
I wanted to be everything from an astronaut to a marine biologist, to a doctor, to a journalist, to a painter (even though I have no artistic skill), to a business woman (whatever that means). Writing was always something I would do alongside of whatever I became. I never wanted to be a teacher, though, and now I'm a college English instructor. It's fair to say, though, that I'm still not sure what I want to be when I grow up.

Shannon Waite

Shannon Waite

Where are you from?
I grew up in Warren, Michigan, which is where I still live to this day. I love the city and this area of the state.

When and why did you begin writing?
Is that even a question? Since I could hold a pencil, I've been writing and drawing. I've always enjoyed creating and I can't remember a time that I wasn't doing it. I'm in love with words, and that fascination has only grown over the years.

What would you say is your most interesting writing quirk?
My most interesting writing quick would have to be poetic prose; I had always written stories when I was younger, and then in high school I focused on poetry. When I transitioned back into storytelling, my poetry bled into the work.

What do you like to do when you're not writing?
If I'm not writing, I'm managing a handful of high schoolers (I'm a teacher), I'm raising hamsters, drinking banana milkshakes, reading, and going on long walks.

As a child, what did you want to do when you grew up?
The list: singer, doctor, vet, writer, president, and probably a few other things. All at once. Then I decided psychologist, and that lasted for four years in high school, then second semester of senior year I vetoed that and decided to be a high school English teacher.

Intrepid Fallen Heroes Fund

The Intrepid Fallen Heroes Fund serves United States military personnel wounded or injured in service to our nation, and their families. Supporting these heroes helps repay the debt all Americans owe them for the sacrifices they have made in service to our nation. They are, in the words of our founder, the late Zachary Fisher, "our nation's greatest national resource," and they deserve all the help that our nation can provide. The Intrepid Fallen Heroes Fund is a leader in meeting this important national mission.

The Intrepid Fallen Heroes Fund is helping military personnel suffering the effects of traumatic brain injury (TBI) and psychological health (PH) conditions by building a series of facilities, called "Intrepid Spirit" centers, in which these injuries can be diagnosed and treated. Hundreds of thousands of military personnel have been diagnosed with TBI or PH conditions and the Intrepid Spirit centers provide the best possible care for these heroes in uniform.

The Intrepid Fallen Heroes Fund does not provide grants or other payments to individuals or organizations. The Fund's sole program is building treatment centers for military personnel suffering the effects of traumatic brain injury and psychological health conditions. The Fund's initial program involved providing grants to families of military personnel lost in performance of their duty, but in 2005 the federal government substantially increased its support for these families, and the Fund then shifted its mission to supporting our nation's wounded heroes.

ONE INTREPID SQUARE · WEST 46TH STREET AND 12TH AVENUE · NEW YORK, NEW YORK 10036   1-800-340-HERO(4376)

http://www.fallenheroesfund.org

www.ingramcontent.com/pod-product-compliance
Lightning Source LLC
Chambersburg PA
CBHW072000170626
46813CB00005B/1951